Raising Mom

Tony Joiner

A YnoT Publishing Book MMXVI

ISBN: 0692696504
ISBN 13: 9780692696507

I'm dedicating this book to all of the single mothers that find a way each and every day to raise their families the best way they know how, regardless of how they came into this situation. I was blessed to be raised by both of my parents, so I've seen this from a distance. Studies show almost 70% of black kids are raised by a single mother for a variety of reasons. Certainly, not all of them are struggling, but many are. We know it's hard enough for a dual parent household, but a single mother has to take on the role of both Father and Mother. Black women have played that role for a long time in some of our neighborhoods; Much love and respect always...

1

SOMEONE'S KNOCKING AT the door. Silence, followed by another knock, this time louder. It's Wednesday night and tomorrow is the first day of school.

"Can someone get the door? I know y'all hear that. DeMario, go open that door, boy!" DeMario gets up from his bed, closes his book, and goes to the front room to open the door. As he looks through the peephole he notices who it is and shakes his head.

"It's Larry. You know who it is, lil' man." DeMario opens the door and lets him in. DeMario looks at him with disgust and turns to head back to his room just as his mother, Teresa, is coming out of hers.

"Mom, why are you with this dude?"

"Boy, don't start with me. Did you iron Carlos clothes like I told you?" Teresa asked.

"Not yet, but tomorrow is the first day of school, and you're going out tonight? I mean, come on."

"Listen boy, I don't answer to you," she says. "Now get yo butt in that room and do what I told you." Markéta, his sister, comes out of her room half dressed, with short shorts on and headed toward the front room. "And where do you think you going dressed like that?" he demands.

"I'm going to the kitchen," says Markéta.

"No way, not with that dude in there dressed like

that." He blocks her path. Marketa rolls her eyes at him and stomps off back to her room. After his mother and her boyfriend leave the house, DeMario goes back to his room with his little brother Carlos, who's now playing video games. "Carlos go take your bath, then it's bedtime. School starts tomorrow," says DeMario.

"Okay," he says, but he hadn't gotten up yet.

"Now!" says his big brother. Carlos finally gets up and goes. The phone rings. "DeMario, the phone is for you," says his youngest sister, Mercedes. "It sounds like yo girlfriend, what's her name, Nicole?!"

"Don't be in my business!" He picks up the phone in his room.

"Hang the phone up, Mercedes!" The phone clicks.

"Hey, what's up? Sorry about that. It's crazy in here. My mom just left with her boyfriend, so I have to get these kids ready for the first day of school."

"Wow, you are busy," says Nicole. "Shouldn't your mom be doing that?"

"Yep. I tried to tell her that. I can't wait to leave here," he groans. "You got it made. You live with both of your parents, you get to see the world since your dad is in the military, and you only have one little brother."

"That's true, but I have to keep up with my studies," says Nicole.

"That's no problem, you're smart." There is a loud

6

knock on his bedroom door. "Who is it?" he shouts. "I'm on the phone!"

"Tell Carlos to get out the shower, he's using all the hot water," says Mercedes. "Hey look, I gotta go. I'll see you tomorrow."

"Okay, bye," says Nicole.

As he leaves the room that he shares with his younger brother, DeMario is thinking, *man it must be nice to live in a nice neighborhood, have some money, and not have to deal with so much drama. Nicole got it good.* He walks to the bathroom door and knocks.

"Carlos, get your behind out the bathroom now or I'm coming in," he shots.

"Okay, I'm drying off, jeez," says Carlos.

"Who drank my soda?" hollers Markéta. "Mercedes, did you drink my soda?"

"I thought it was Mama's. You left it in her room," says Mercedes.

"Yes, because I had to get something out of her room."

"Well, I guess next time you won't leave it," says Mercedes, as she races out the room.

"Hey, what are you guys doing in Mom's room? You know she doesn't want you in here when she's gone." says DeMario. He didn't want them snooping around in the bedroom because he knew his Mom kept her pistol and her marijuana in there.

Their living condition wasn't the best. They lived in a low-income neighborhood. There were always drug dealers, shootings, people getting robbed and also loud music throughout the night.

Teresa had DeMario when she was still in high school and less than a year later she had Marketa. DeMario and Marketa have the same dad. Both Mercedes and Carlos have different dads.

Mercedes' dad always help and supports the other children. Carlos' dad was originally from Mexico and he worked at the same place as their mother. The family mostly relied on one income and some assistance from the government. Teresa worked as a housekeeper at the military base lodging. She had been laid off twice; once for drugs, and once for being late to work because of car trouble. She also did hair on the side even though she wasn't licensed.

2

TONIGHT, TERESA WAS with her latest male friend, Larry, whom she had met at a club. They had been together for a few weeks. He owns a lawn service business and tonight he was taking her to an old school R&B club, her favorite type of music to listen to. They ordered some drinks.

"So, when are you going to spend the night over my place?" he asked.

"Look, for now we are just kicking it and having fun. Remember, no strings. We do what we do when we are together, let's keep it that way. Man, you want me to spend a whole night with you tonight and leave my kids at home knowing school starts tomorrow?" Then she added, "They already don't want me to be with you, especially my oldest two. You already know that."

"Fine, okay, but you make it hard on a brother. Cat like me don't wait forever."

"Look, you want to take me back home? You messing with my high."

"Girl, you know I'm kidding," he says grinning at her. Teresa looked him in the eye and says, "Yeah, right," and turned her head.

Back at home, the kids were preparing for the first day of school.

"What are you wearing tomorrow?" DeMario asked

Markéta. "It better not be tight."

"Boy, you are not my dad."

"You right, however, you won't be leaving here if it is, I bet you that."

"Whatever," is her response with a snap of her finger.

"Do you want those guys to be looking at you like some skank?"

"Can't stop them from looking."

"You just don't get it, do you?"

"No, you don't get it," she says.

"Do you want to get pregnant and end up like Mama? I am not babysitting yo kids."

"I'm going to tell Mama what you said," says Markéta.

"Tell her it's the truth," he says as he walks away. The phone rings again. "Who can it be now?" Looking at the caller ID it was their Great Aunt Janice asking to speak to Teresa. "She's not here, Aunt Janice," says DeMario. "She's gone out with Larry somewhere."

"Oh, okay, I'll call her tomorrow. School starts tomorrow, don't it?"

"Yes, ma'am,"

"This is your last year, isn't it? You ready to leave school aren't you? I know you are."

"Yes, ma'am."

"Well, don't be in too big of a hurry. Once you old, you ain't never young again." She started laughing. Aunt Janice asked him about some tomatoes and peppers that they were growing in their garden.

"I will tell Mama to bring you some."

Aunt Janice was their great-aunt. She was older than their grandmother and lived across town. She has no children of her own. They loved to go to her house just to hear her talk and listen to her tell about the good ole days with their Grandmother. Later that night, while resting in bed, DeMario heard his mother arriving home. He thought to himself, *I hope it was worth it*.

3

THE NEXT MORNING the kids are getting ready for school. Teresa is cooking breakfast.

"Don't think I'm cooking every morning. Mercedes and Carlos eat breakfast at school and besides we got cereal." She turned to DeMario. "D, make sure Markéta get out of here on time." Sometimes they called him D for short. The two youngest kids rode a different bus than DeMario and Markéta.

"Hey, where are my cigarettes? D, did you hide my smokes? Boy, don't play with me."

"They are probably in the car where you left them," DeMario sighs.

"I don't want to get no calls from the principal this year, y'all hear me?" Markéta starts snickering.

"You're the one I'm talking about Markéta, getting in fights and talking back." Markéta rolls her eyes as she usually does when her mom says things like this about her.

Markéta has a lot in common with her mom. They are both headstrong and hate to be told what to do. They always got the attention of the guys. Teresa even told Markéta once, "You stole my body!" which made both of them laugh. Markéta loved the attention she got and it made her feel good. In most instances, she was the queen bee, and her friends followed her lead. She was now a cheerleader just like her mother Teresa was.

This didn't sit too well with DeMario. He didn't like the idea of the guys at school gawking at his little sister and asking him questions about her. After everyone had left except DeMario and Markéta, he checked all the doors and windows to make sure that they were locked. "Girl come on out here, the bus will be at the corner in a minute or two."

"Boy, I'm coming," she yells back.

As they are leaving the house, the phone rings.

"Who could be calling now?" says DeMario.

"It could be mom calling about something," says Markéta. After reopening the door and checking the caller ID, the call was not their mother. "Hello?"

"Hello, is Miss Teresa in?"

"No, she's at work, who is this?"

"This is the Health and Wellness Clinic, she didn't come in for her test results last Friday or call. Have her call as soon as she can," says the caller.

"What kind of test was it?" asks DeMario.

"We don't give out that information. Just have her call. Goodbye."

"Who was it?" asked Markéta.

"The health clinic says they have the test results for mom. What kind of test did she take?" Then DeMario tells his sister. "Hope it isn't some stupid STD or something like that."

"Why you always think that way?" says Markéta. "You ain't no better than nobody."

"I'm just saying, all those different boyfriends over the years."

13

"Boy, you need to shut your mouth up about my Mama." says Markéta.

As they are walking toward the bus stop, a car driven by the twins, Isaac and Isaiah slows down and ask them if they want a ride, especially Markéta. "Hey, Isaac and Isaiah," says Markéta.

"Naw man, not today," says DeMario.

"Okay, see y'all on the yard," says Isaac as they drive away.

"Man, I wish we had a car to drive to school in," says Markéta.

"Me too, that's why I got to get a job," says DeMario.

"How you going to get a job and play ball at the same time?" asked Markéta.

"I'm thinking about getting a part-time job working at that sub shop down the street. How hard can it be to fix some sandwiches? Anyway, baseball season hasn't started yet."

They get to the bus stop just in time as it is pulling up. "If we were any later..."

Before DeMario can finish the sentence Markéta says, "But we ain't!"

They get on the bus with the rest of the kids. Everybody's laughing and joking, checking out the new gear that everyone has on. DeMario is sitting with his friend Michael Brown, better known as Big Mike because there is another Michael Brown in the neighborhood and that's how they distinguish the two.

"Man, we got one more year to go and we are out of here, yo," says Mike.

"Man, you better know it," says DeMario. He sniffs the air. "You smell weed?"

"Yep," responds Mike.

"Okay, who is firing up a blunt this early in the morning?" somebody asks.

Someone else interrupted. "Y'all know who it probably is, Shirley."

"Sho is," says Shirley.

Shirley's brother was a known drug dealer, so it was no problem for her to get high. He had been in and out of jail many times for drug-related crimes. He was known around the neighborhood as Stackman because his favorite phrase was, *'Stacking that paper'*. DeMario sometimes wondered if that was who his mom got her drugs from, although he had never seen her buy any.

Once they reach the school yard, they all get off the bus. DeMario and Marketa head toward their separate homerooms. "Hey, don't forget I have cheerleading practice, so Mom will pick me up. I won't be on the bus."

"I know, I know," says DeMario. Once he gets into homeroom he sees Nicole. They have two classes together. He leans toward her and whispers in her ear. "Hey girl, what's up?"

She giggles and says, "You aren't that cool."

"Yes, I am, and you know it," he says. The school bell rings so DeMario goes to his seat.

Marketa, as usual, has her mind on anything but her class work. She's a smart student. Although, she's not as smart as DeMario, especially not in math. She sometimes gets help from him. She hasn't always done her best, sometimes just enough to stay above average, but this year she needs to maintain a high-grade point average to go to a good college. That's her dream.

She wants to get into a sorority and enjoy all the glitz and glamor that comes with it. As she sits in her English class, she thinks about her mom who had the same ideas; finish high school, go to a historically black college, join a sorority. After getting pregnant with DeMario, that all changed. Four kids and three baby daddies later, she's working on a military base as a housekeeper. Markéta wants none of that.

After his first three classes, DeMario seeks out Nicole during their lunch break. He gets his food and sits next to her. "So, how's it going so far?"

"Can you believe we have homework on the first day of school?" she stated. They are in the same science class.

"Insane," he expressed. "Miss Armstrong is known for giving lots of homework in her science class. I see why she is a misses, she has the perfect last name; Armstrong." He smiles as he expresses joy.

"That's not right," says Nicole. "Hey, you haven't seen my car yet." She shows him a picture of her car on her cellphone.

"A VW beetle. Nice, it's fit you."

"Hey, you want a ride home after school?"

"Naw, maybe some other time."

"Why? Is it because of where you live?"

"No," says DeMario in a raised voice.

"Why then? You're not playing football this year, so

you won't be staying after school, so that's not it." He wanted to change the subject, so he asked her. "Why didn't you try out for cheerleading?"

"Are you kidding? My parents would kill me. Wearing all those skimpy tights and having people look at you as if you were on a menu. At least that's what my Mom says. I would have loved to be one, but don't tell my parents," she laughs.

As they are eating Markéta and her followers walk by with their food. "Hey Nicole, I don't see what you see in him," says Markéta as she shakes her head and continues to her table.

"I do," says one of her friends.

"Hey, don't listen to them," says DeMario. Some of Markéta's male friends were also sitting with her and her friends being very noisy.

"I can see you don't like who she hangs with, do you?"

"Explain this to me, why would you desire to be with people that are a lot of backstabbers? Those same individuals will go home, get on the phone, and talk about each other. I just don't get it." The bell rings. "I'll see you later," says DeMario as he grabs his backpack.

"All right," says Nicole as she maneuvers to her next class.

4

MEANWHILE ACROSS TOWN at the base lodging, Teresa is making up a bed when Chantel, one of the other housekeepers and her best friend, comes in.

"Hey girl. How's the new man working out?"

"What new man? You mean Larry?" She stops making up the bed. "Look, I've only been out with him a few times, that's all. You already know that."

"Right, okay if you say so."

"I don't have to lie to you, Chantel."

"So, you never told me what DeMario thinks about him."

"What he always thinks about every guy I bring home; he hates him. The only guy he never complains about is Marcus."

"Girl, you got to live yo own life. Sometimes you need a man, I'm just saying," remarked Chantel.

"You know, that's how I got those kids, needing a man," says Teresa. As she's talking, Chantel notices a watch on the floor.

"That last guy left his watch." She picks it up from under a chair. "It looks expensive too."

"Let me see it. It was a colonel in here," says Teresa. "He left yesterday, and he hasn't called back to check on it."

"I'd be taking it to the pawn shop today if it was me. Look what the guy down the hall left me." She went to her cart and pulled out two beers. "He says he didn't have time to drink them, so he left them in the room want one?"

"You know I do ... close the door." They quickly drank the beers inside the room.

"Now I need a smoke break."

"Girl me too," responded Teresa. They congregate with other housekeepers along with the maintenance guys. They all share the same smoking area.

"I heard there's going to be a new drug policy," says Darlene, one of the housekeepers.

"Yep, they are trying to weed some of us out," says Chantel. "And besides that, they think there are too many of us as it is."

Will Sherman, a maintenance guy, replies in a tiresome and matter of fact voice. "Well, you know some of us got the inside track on that."

"So, Will, what are you trying to say?" They all knew what he meant. Will was talking about Hector, Carlos father. The word was that's how she manages to keep her job. Hector was the supervisor over maintenance, the position Will thought he was going to get.

"Chantel, I don't need you to speak up for me," says Teresa, as she turns toward Will. "And Will, you need to keep yo mouth off me and mine, that's why you so lonely now. You talk more than a woman."

"I bet he ain't even seeing that boy," says Will.

"Will, you better move on," says Darlene. Teresa was getting very upset so Chantel, Darlene, and the other housekeepers pulled her away from the situation and headed back to work. Teresa was still angry about what had just happened. Did other co-workers feel the same way? She had a short relationship with Hector when they were working together in the same building. They both knew it wasn't going anywhere, besides, he was already married, and she had no intentions of marrying him anyway. She hadn't intended to get pregnant. If kids only knew how and where they were conceived, she thought.

5

BACK AT THE school, DeMario was in his last class when he was called to the office. He had no idea what it was for. Was something wrong? Had something happened to someone in his family? His mind was racing. As he entered the office, he was told to see the counselor. Mrs. Jones, the counselor, told him to be seated. Someone wanted to see him. *Who would want to see him on the first day of school?* Mrs. Jones made small talk, asking him how everything was going. There was a knock on the door.

"Come in," says Mrs. Jones. A tall man enters the office. He had a big grin on his face as he looked at DeMario.

"Is this the young man?" he says, looking from Mrs. Jones to DeMario.

"Yes, sir, it is," she says. The man holds out his hand to DeMario. He grasps it and the man shakes his hand vigorously.

"Great to meet you! My name is Mr. Greenleaf. I gather you are probably wondering who I am."

"Yes, sir."

"Well, I'll leave and let you two get acquainted," says Mrs. Jones. She walks out of the room and closes the door behind her.

"I'm a recruiter for Stedman University. Stedman would love to have a young man with your grades attend our school on a full scholarship! If you can maintain your grades, of course. How does that sound?"

21

Wow! thought DeMario. He had no idea that any school of this caliber was interested in him. He had sent out information to respective schools during the summertime, but this was unexpected.

"Mr. Greenleaf, sir, this is all new to me. I never applied to Stedman. How did you guys come across me, if I may ask?"

"Sure! We saw your remarkable ACT score. We followed up by taking a look at your grades. That's how we made the decision to offer you the scholarship." As Mr. Greenleaf was talking about the scholarship and the school, DeMario was thinking, finally, after all that studying and missing out on parties and other things, he was getting a break.

"Can I get back to you at a later date?" says DeMario. "This is my first offer. I will have to speak to my mom about it."

"That's what I expected you to say. This is a big decision and I'm sure you will be getting other offers, but remember we were first," says Mr. Greenleaf with a smile on his face.

"Here's my information and the schools' website is also on this card," he continued. "By the way, what would you want to major in?"

"I want to major in engineering," says DeMario.

"We have one of the best engineering schools in the country," says Mr. Greenleaf. "Stedman University would be a great fit for you, but I am a little biased. Here, a few gifts for you." He hands DeMario a bag with a tee shirt and other items with the school logo and colors on it. "I look forward to speaking with you soon, DeMario." Mr. Greenleaf shakes his hand again and leaves the office. As DeMario heads out the door, Mrs. Jones calls him back to her office. "Yes, Mrs. Jones?"

"So, what do you think about what just happened?"

"I believe that it is an excellent opportunity to get a free education. Now my mom or I won't have to worry about it."

"I'm certain this is only the start," says Mrs. Jones. "There will be others to come. You will have to determine which is better for you. Opportunities like this don't come around often."

DeMario knew she was right, people in his neighborhood didn't get chances like this too often. It would have been nice to get an athletic scholarship, but it's even better to get an academic scholarship.

After receiving this news, DeMario decided that he would accept that drive home from Nicole. After retrieving his belongings from his locker, he went to the student parking lot where he found her about to leave. He flagged her down.

"Hey, wait up, can I still get that ride?"

"So, what changed your mind?" she says, as he was getting into the car.

"This is really nice; the color fits you," says DeMario, referring to the car. "Why don't you let the top down?"

"I only do it on the weekend."

"Let me guess, dads' decision?"

"No, actually it's my decision, and you still haven't

answered my question. What changed your mind?" insisted Nicole.

"I just got a scholarship offer."

"That's great! For baseball?"

"No, for academics, from Stedman University. That's what I was called to the office for."

"How cool is that," says Nicole as she was driving off campus.

"I'll have to show you where I live," says DeMario.

"Actually, I already know where you live."

"How do you know that?"

"I looked it up on the Internet once before and drove by there."

After hearing this DeMario was now staring at Nicole as if she had kept a secret from him.

"Are you mad?" *Why would she do that?*

"No," he says.

"It certainly sounds like you are mad."

"I said no, didn't I?"

"So, I know where you live, what's wrong with that?"

"You just wouldn't understand. Where I live, I hate it. Don't you look at the news? Just last week a little kid I knew was killed at the park by a stray bullet."

Nicole could tell by his tone that DeMario was frustrated by the situation. "Didn't you just get a scholarship offer?" says Nicole. "And you are from the so-called hood. Everything from the hood isn't all bad, so stop talking like that."

"Okay already. So, how many schools have offered you a scholarship?"

"Um, I think I have about five and I'm sure my mom has a few more she wants to look into."

"That's cool to have your parents to help you out with all this."

"Yeah, I guess. Sometimes it can be overbearing. You know she didn't want me to have a car until after graduation, but my father stepped in and saved the day."

"My Mom is so busy doing other stuff. I feel like a dad sometimes when it comes to taking care of things around the house and doing for my sisters and brother," says DeMario.

After they made it to DeMario's house. His younger sister and brother were playing outside next door. They were over their neighbors' house, Ms. Lillie. That's where they stayed after school until someone came home. After seeing DeMario, Carlos and Mercedes run over to meet him.

"Who car is this and who are you?" Carlos says pointing at Nicole.

"That's Nicole," says Mercedes.

"Stop being so nosy. Here is the key. I'll be in there in a minute, go." As the kids head into the house Nicole looks at DeMario and says "Umm, is that your brother? He looks a little different than the rest of y'all to me."

"That's because his dad is Latino. Oh, I never told you that before?"

"I think I would have remembered that. Wow, your

mom doesn't discriminate."

"Look, don't talk that way about my mom."

"I didn't mean it the way it sounded. I'm sorry if I offended you," says Nicole.

"Yeah, I know. People often look at him and you can imagine what they are saying. After a while, you get used to it. Those little girls are always looking at him. It's cool. He loves the attention," he says. "You know I forgot to have you drop me off at that sandwich shop to get an application."

"Want to go back?"

"Naw, that's okay. I'll probably do it this weekend. Thanks for the ride. I'll call you later tonight."

"All right then," says Nicole.

6

TERESA AND THE housekeeping crew were all standing around waiting to clock out when Hector pulls up in a golf cart and motions her to come over.

"Hector, what do you want?"

"Look, I'm just giving you the heads up about that new drug policy."

"You don't need to worry about me. I'm already aware of that." She looks back to see who is paying attention to them. "By the way, don't forget that Carlos birthday is coming up and that money you gave me for his school doesn't count as a birthday present."

"Look Teresa, I'm barely making ends meet."

"Hector, I don't want to hear that. Is that what you want me to tell Carlos? That your dad can't get you a birthday present because he has no money, really?"

"Come on, Teresa." says Hector as he attempts to rub her leg and says something in Spanish.

"Hector, I'm not flirting with you." She gives a mild grin. "Don't even try that Spanish talk with me."

"Okay. Voy a hablar con usted más tarde."

"See, I told you about that." As she walks away and looks at him she wonders why she allowed herself to get with him in the first place. She already knew the answer. It wasn't all his fault. It was the attention that she was always getting from him and others like him. It was like a dangerous game she would play, having unprotected sex with guys, then worry about it later. How stupid, she thought. As she was heading back toward the group she saw Will Sherman looking at her and shaking his head as if he didn't approve of her being with Hector. He can shake his head all he wants, she thought. If she gave him the chance she knew he would come running. Maybe that's the issue. Maybe in his mind, he was wondering why she never showed any interest in him or the other guys at work. As she prepared to clock out she remembered that she had to pick up Markéta from school.

"Hey girl, what was Hector talking about?" Chantel was standing behind her getting ready to clock out.

"The same old stuff. Trying not to get Carlos something for his birthday, but girl you know I'm not going for that."

"Girl, they are altogether the same. Excuses, apologies, and more excuses," says Chantel as she clocks out. "You coming by tonight? You know we got the card game going on."

"You know I am, gotta get my drink on," remarks Teresa. She snaps her fingers. "See you later, I have to pick up Markéta from cheerleading practice."

"Oh, by the way, are you bringing Larry with you?"

"Stop playing. You don't bring sand to the beach."

"See, that's how you get in trouble,"

"I know right."

Teresa gets into her car and lights up a cigarette. She turns the radio on while she checks her messages on her cell phone. One is from the clinic, which closes in about fifteen minutes, so she decides to give them a call as she drives toward the schoolyard to pick up Markéta. The results of her STD test are negative. After hearing this, she gives a sigh of relief. Again, she has managed to get lucky. She can't keep doing this. Once she arrives at the schoolyard, she sees Markéta talking to one of the twins. Markéta sees her, then she whispers something to Isaiah before making her way to the car.

"Hey, Mom," says Markéta.

"What are you and that boy talking about? Which one is he?"

"That one is Isaiah."

"I didn't know he played football."

"He didn't, this will be his first year for both him and his brother."

"So, what were you whispering in his ear?"

"Mom don't be so nosy."

"I ain't trying to raise no grandkids."

"Mom!" says Markéta.

"You heard me," says Teresa.

"See, now you are tripping."

One of Teresa favorite Isley Brothers songs comes on the radio causing Teresa to start moving to the beat, forgetting her and Markéta's conversation. "That's my song right there!"

"How many favorite songs you got?" says Markéta.

"Youngster, don't trip. These are real songs, not all this rap y'all listen to," says Teresa.

"Mom, sometimes you listen to rap too." Teresa just kept on singing as if she didn't hear Markéta, as they make their way home.

7

DEMARIO IS IN the kitchen helping his younger brother and sister when they hear the car pull up outside. Carlos looks out the window and says, "Mom and Markéta are here."

"Good, I'm hungry," says Mercedes.

"You just had a sandwich," says DeMario.

"Yeah, a peanut butter sandwich."

"Hey, Mom," says Mercedes.

"My little precious. How was the first day of school?"

"It was fine, but I have homework to do."

"Some of her homework requires the Internet, so I'll have to use your phone," says DeMario. Teresa's phone was the only Internet access that they had in the home.

"Mom, you said you were going to get internet service," Mercedes says.

"Have to get a computer first," says DeMario.

"I think she knows that dodo," says Markéta shaking her head at DeMario.

Carlos hands his mother some paperwork about the Cub Scouts. "Mom, can I be in the Cub Scouts?"

"Carlos baby, I can't afford for you to be in the Cub Scouts. That cost money, maybe next year."

The telephone rings. DeMario picks it up. It's Uncle Nate, Teresa's older brother who's in the Army. He often calls to see how they are doing.

"What's up, nephew?"

"Nothing much, Unk. Today was the first day of school. Are you still stationed in Colorado?"

"Yeah man, I love it because of the scenery. I may stay here after I retire. You still playing sports?"

"Yep, this year I'm just going to play baseball so that I can concentrate more on my studies. I just got offered a full scholarship today."

"Man, that's fantastic, for baseball?"

"Naw, academics."

After overhearing the conversation, Teresa asks, "You got offered a scholarship and didn't tell me?"

"Mama, you didn't give me a chance to tell you, you just got home."

"So, you told Nate about the scholarship before you told me, wow!" Uncle Nate could hear her in the background, so he tells DeMario to put her on the phone.

"Teresa, why you tripping? Didn't you just get home? You need to stop that."

"I still don't understand why he told you first. I'm glad he got a scholarship offer," says Teresa.

"Teresa, it's not like he was going to keep it a secret. Now put him back on the phone, and you go and calm down."

"Look, Nate, you don't tell me to calm down, I ain't got started yet. Here, come get this phone," says Teresa, handing the phone back to DeMario. "You know I'm proud of you, don't you?"

"Yes ma'am, I know," says DeMario. He heads toward his bedroom. "Hey Unk, I'm back. Man, Mama be tripping sometimes."

"I know, I know, but you know she means well. She's always had a strong will even back in the day, but anyway, guess what I picked up the other day?"

"What you got, Unk?"

"A Trans Am. One of the officers on base had to let it go. He says he had to pay for his daughter's college, so he sold it to me. It needs a little interior and exterior work, but nothing I can't fix," insisted his uncle. "Hey, what's your email address? I can send you pictures right now."

"We don't have a computer or the internet."

"Man, y'all don't have a computer? How can you do your homework?" questioned Uncle Nate. "The internet is a must nowadays."

"I usually have to do it at school or somewhere else."

"Listen here young blood, let big Uncle take care of this right now. Once we get off the phone I'm going to order you a laptop, top of the line, and have it sent to you."

"Unk, are you for real?" says DeMario.

"Listen nephew, I don't have any kids and I'm not married, so money ain't a thang when it comes to my nieces and nephews."

DeMario knew this to be true. Anytime they were in a tight spot, Uncle Nate would always help out. He knew that it was a struggle sometimes for Teresa. "By the way, you have to let your sisters and brother use it if they need to. Come Christmas when I come down there I'll buy a desktop computer, so you guys can put it in the front room. I'll see to it that Teresa gets the internet. D, you should have called and told me before now that you needed a computer."

"I know. I was hoping to have a part-time job by now."

"Don't let a job keep you from your studies or those little girls," says Uncle Nate with a chuckle. DeMario knew eventually Uncle Nate would get around to the girls. It was his way of trying to find out if he had a girlfriend or not.

"Naw, man I ain't going to let that happen. I got me a shorty, she cool."

"I hear you, nephew!"

"So, Uncle Nate, why didn't you ever get married or have kids, if you don't mind me asking?"

"Naw, D, I don't mind you asking, it wasn't my intention not to have those things. Once my career got going with all the moving, being down range, and the different schools it just made it easier for me not to have to worry about family. I love what I do, but it's winding down now, so who knows."

"Uncle Nate, you been all over the world."

"That's right, in some cases three or four times. See DeMario, I always had a goal that I had to get out of the situation that I was born into. As a black man it would have been easy for me to have given up or make excuses for myself, that's why I know you can do it, so don't get discouraged or let any situation get you down. Excuses don't put food on your table or clothes on your back. I went from being a private to a Major." DeMario loved it when Uncle Nate drops down some knowledge. "Look here young fella, let me holla at my other nieces and nephew. You hang in there, now, you hear me? And don't let them little girls run you crazy, boy," says Uncle Nate with a laugh.

"Ok, Uncle Nate," says DeMario. He goes to the front room and gives the phone to Mercedes then goes back to his room. About an hour later, DeMario could smell dinner being prepared in the kitchen. When he got to the kitchen, dinner was almost ready. Markéta had made her favorite dish; homemade macaroni and cheese with some string beans. His mom had baked fish and some rolls.

"Mom says she's going to Chantel's house tonight," says Markéta looking at DeMario, knowing how he would feel about that idea.

"Mom, this evening? I can't help everybody with their homework, then do mine, and still do my chores," says DeMario, shaking his head in disbelief. "These are your kids, not mine."

"Boy, who do you think you're talking to?" demanded Teresa. "I know whose kids these are." Teresa is now standing up from the table. "None of your dads are here, not one, so don't tell me who's kids these are." DeMario now felt uneasy about his previous statement.

"Mom, nobody said anything about our dads. I'm sorry for what I said. I know you work hard to put food on the table, clothes on our back, and all that stuff."

"Don't you think I know what day it is?" says Teresa looking around the table at her offspring.

"Mom, it's just that it was the first day of school and we think you should stay home tonight," says Markéta. "And you said you were going to finish up with our forms so we can

35

turn them in tomorrow."

Teresa could see the concern on her children's faces. They thought that she was going out too much and spending less time with them lately. Carlos, her youngest, was now in the third grade, Mercedes the fifth, Marketa a junior, and DeMario a senior. Was she trying to make up for the time she lost after having kids, like parties and having fun with her friends?

"Look, I'm sorry if you guys think that way. Maybe I do need to stay home tonight. I went out last night anyway. Just remember, I need some down time too. I worked six days straight last week, okay?"

"Sure, Mom," says Mercedes.

Teresa turns to DeMario and slaps him across the head gently. "So DeMario, are you going to tell me about that scholarship?" DeMario tells Teresa about the scholarship and what was mentioned by the recruiter as he does his kitchen chores. "It sounds good. At least I won't have to find a way to pay for your college," says Teresa. "What about baseball? What if you get a chance to play; are you going to take it or go to school?"

"I don't know right now."

"Why aren't you playing football this year anyway?"

"Mom, I told you, so I can concentrate more on my studies. I'm better at baseball."

"Yeah, but you can get to the pros quicker," says Teresa. DeMario just stopped talking. He knew she really wanted him to play football or basketball. It was more popular to play those sports, especially in his neighborhood.

After the homework was done and all the chores, everyone retreats to his or her room. Teresa goes outside to smoke a cigarette. She gets a call from Chantel asking her why she isn't at the party.

"Tonight isn't a good night. The kids wanted me to stay at home, so I gave in. Maybe they are right. I have been going out on the regular lately."

"Did you hear from Larry tonight?"

"I'm surprised he hasn't called me today. Must be doing something he has no business doing. I'll see you tomorrow and let you know if he calls," says Teresa.

"Oh, what did you do with that watch?" asked Chantel.

"I still have it, I'll wait a few days and decide what to do with it. What if he calls and I already pawned it? I'll let you know," says Teresa.

8

THE FOLLOWING WEEKS are relatively routine. The kids are back in school taking care of their studies. DeMario got his laptop in the mail from Uncle Nate who also paid for the internet service. Marketá is enjoying the spotlight of being a cheerleader.

Mercedes and Carlos are still tattling on each other about something or another. Teresa is seeing Larry on and off, which depends on how she feels at any given time. The idea of calling him her boyfriend is something she is not ready to do just yet. If she wants to see someone else she doesn't want to feel as though she is cheating on him. She wants to be able to do as she pleases without looking over her shoulder or feeling sorry about it. After all, she is a grown, single, and free woman.

9

G A M E   D A Y   H A S finally arrived and Markéta is very excited as they get ready for school. She packs all her gear in her cheerleading bag and makes sure everybody knows tonight is her night.

"Mom, today you don't have to pick me up from school. I'm staying at the school till after the game, but I do need some money."

"I know. You told me a thousand times already." Teresa gives Markéta some money. "I remember those days, so I know the feeling. We will be there rooting you on."

"Mom, we're going to the game too right?" says Carlos.

"Of course, I got to see my little girl perform, although I'm sure they can't compete with the old school."

"Ahh Mom," says Markéta. Carlos asks DeMario was he going to the game.

"I'll be there."

"Are you going with us?"

"No, I'm going with someone else."

"That girl who was in the car that day?"

"Yep, I will be going with her."

"D, you coming home first?" asks Teresa. "Someone needs to be here when the kids get home from school."

"Yeah Mom, she's picking me up here," says DeMario.

"By the way, Marcus is supposed to come by and pick

39

up Mercedes and take her shopping before the game," says Teresa. Marcus is Mercedes dad who's single and has an automobile shop. He constantly sees to it that Mercedes has what she needs. DeMario thinks Marcus is an okay guy. He has no problem with him and on some occasions has even called him up for advice.

DeMario and Markéta's dad was shot down in a drug deal gone wrong six months after Markéta was born. After learning about this from Aunt Janice when they were younger, neither DeMario nor Markéta has ever brought it up around their mother.

10

AFTER EVERYONE LEAVES for school, Teresa breathes a sigh of relief. She plans to thoroughly enjoy her day off. She didn't even tell the kids she was off. She goes to her bedroom and opens her bottom drawer and takes out a bag of marijuana. While she's rolling up a joint, she thinks about the new drug testing policy at work and how stupid it was for her to take a chance like this. *This will be my last joint*, she thought.

She goes outside to the backyard and continues to smoke. While waiting for Larry to show up, she starts pruning the tomato plants. He is supposed to come by to see her once the kids are off to school.

Teresa notices the butterflies flying around as she is working in her garden. She remembers as a child they would try to catch them and put them in a jug. She always had a thing for them. She had pictures of butterflies throughout her house.

About thirty minutes later, Larry shows up. She has him come around to the backyard.

"Puff, puff, pass," says Larry when he sees Teresa smoking the joint.

"Some things I share; this ain't one of them," says Teresa.

"Wow girl, why you so hard on a brother?"

"I don't know where yo mouth been."

"That's funny. Well, can I get one?"

"Look in that bag," says Teresa pointing to a plastic bag under a lawn chair.

"Are we drinking anything?" asks Larry as he rolls up a joint.

"Why, so you can be drinking and driving and kill someone?"

"No, just one beer, besides, I will sweat it out. I have four more yards to landscape on this side of town and my guys are handling that," he says. He makes his way into the house and comes out with a beer in one hand and a joint in the other.

"You know the first game of the season is tonight. Are you coming?" asks Teresa.

"With you?" asks Larry. He takes a drink. "You know your kids don't want me there. I'll probably be by later after the game."

"You know Markéta is a cheerleader and she can't wait till tonight."

"Just like her mama. Okay, okay, I'll see what I can do."

11

MIDWAY THRU THE school day Markéta and the cheerleaders along with several volunteers are preparing for the first game tonight with banners and posters scattered around the campus. The pep rally will begin right after the last class. All extracurricular participants were allowed to leave early to prepare. Markéta was in the gymnasium along with the rest of the cheerleaders finishing up when she heard her name called.

"Hey Markéta. Y'all got it going on." It was Isaiah.

"Boy, y'all better win tonight."

"You know we are going to show up. You can bet that."

Markéta knew that Isaiah liked her, and she had always liked him too, but they never really let it get any further than just being friends up until this point.

"So, what are your plans after the game?"

"Don't know. My mom will probably take me home or I will ride with Vanessa."

"Hey, if you want to come by Graffiti's that's where most of us will be."

"Okay, see you there."

Graffiti's was a place where most of the students went after games. It had a dance floor, game room, and also served food.

DeMario was alone in the science lab, putting the finishing touch on his science project. The science teacher, Miss Armstrong comes in and compliments him on his project.

"So DeMario, what are your future plans?" She sits down in the seat next to him. "You know you are one of my best students. The fact that you are here proves my point."

"I'm leaning towards engineering."

"That's wonderful. What type of engineering?"

"I'm not sure right now. I'm looking at ceramic or environmental," says DeMario.

"In some way, I'm not surprised at either one of those options. Have you discussed any of this with your mother?"

"A little, but not much."

"You know your mom was a smart student too. Teresa was a smart girl."

"I know she was smart in math. She tells me all the time that's where I get it from."

"Is she still headstrong? I haven't seen her in a while."

"Most people would say yes to that question."

The school bell rings. The students and faculty head toward the gymnasium. On his way, DeMario catches up with Nicole. "Are you ready for tonight?"

"Sure, and you? I know your sister is," says Nicole. "I'm still picking you up at your house, right?"

"Yep, I have to be there for my little brother and sister."

"Want me to drop you off after school?"

"No, that's okay, I'll ride the bus so you won't have to use all that gas."

"How did your interview go on yesterday?"

"I think it went pretty good." DeMario had an

interview at the sandwich shop.

"Maybe I should get an application. What do you think about that?"

"Sure, why not," says DeMario.

Once the students have filed in for the pep rally the music is blaring. The students are cheering as the cheerleaders escort the football players into their position on the basketball court. The cheerleaders do their thing and the band is playing its rendition of the latest songs. DeMario can see his sister is having a good time and not missing a beat or a cheer. He knows she has worked really hard to get to this point. It was always her dream to be a cheerleader.

Different speakers address the students. DeMario pulled out a letter he received in the mail this morning; it's another scholarship offer. This time it's an athletic scholarship offer for baseball to play at Stiles University. Stiles is one of the top five schools for baseball in the country. More options. The more options he has, the harder the decision will be. He thought it should be easier with more options, but no.

After the pep rally is over and the students are let go, DeMario heads toward the locker room to speak to his sister. Once Markéta sees him she puts a big smile on her face.

"Did you see us? We nailed all the cheers, and no one messed up."

"Don't hate, you know we were good."
"Yeah, it was okay," says DeMario with a smirk on his face. "How are you getting home today?"

"I'm riding with Vanessa." Vanessa was also a cheerleader who lived not too far from them.

"Okay, just checking. Later."

The students file out of the gymnasium and head toward the busses. DeMario glances at the student parking all decked out in the school colors. It would be nice to have a car of his own, even an old beat up one, he thought. On the way home on the bus, Big Mike asks him if he's going to the game tonight. "Yeah, I'm going with Nicole. She's going to pick me up."

"Must be nice. Do her parents know where you live?"

After hearing the question, DeMario thought about it. It never occurred to him to ask her did her parents knew where he lived. He hadn't even met them.

"Man, I don't even know. When she picks me up tonight I'll ask her." The bus rounds the corner. DeMario sees two cars over his house. One is his mom and the other is Marcus there to pick up Mercedes. Once he is off the bus and is walking toward the house he sees Marcus and his mother talking. He would much rather see her with him than those other guys, especially Larry.

"What's up, my good man?" says Marcus.

"School, man, just gotta finish this year out." They give each other the close fist tap.

"So, what's up, you getting Mercedes?" says DeMario.

"Yeah." DeMario sees Mercedes coming out of the house.

"She's been bad too," he says with a grin.

46

"He's lying, don't listen to him," Mercedes responds.

"Hey, I'll take Carlos too if your mom doesn't mind." Marcus is looking directly at Teresa as he is saying that.

"Marcus, don't start. What am I going to say to that? Just have them back in time for the game."

"Catch you guys in a couple of hours," says Marcus. The three of them get into Marcus' car and ride away.

"You're home early. You get off early today?"

"No, today was my off day, I just didn't tell you guys."

"Oh ok. Did you say Markéta could ride with Vanessa?"

"Yes, she called me on my phone."

"Hey, guess what? I got another scholarship offer, this time from Stiles University for baseball."

"Seems I won't have to pay for your college. God knows I don't have the money. You just better keep those grades up." She then grabs a cigarette from her purse and heads to the back porch.

DeMario follows her outside.

"Mom, how long have you been smoking cigarettes? Since high school?"

"DeMario, son, not today," she sighs. "I know you mean well, but sometimes I don't want to hear it and today is one of those times."

"Okay, but let me say this. Don't you want to be around long enough to see all of us graduate high school, college, and have our own families? We want you to be around for that, I'm just saying." DeMario looked over from the lawn chair he was sitting on and noticed what looks like the end of a marijuana bud on the ground. He picks up what's left of the joint and tosses it into the trash. "Mom, you been smoking pot? What if Mercedes and Carlos saw that?"

"D, what if they did, I'm a grown woman. I only keep it away from them because of you and Markéta." DeMario knew this to be true. Their mother only kept it from the younger kids because they asked her to. DeMario was unaware of the implications Teresa's smoking pot would have on her job if she failed a drug test.

12

MEANWHILE, MARKÉTA AND Vanessa was on their way to the mall to get something to eat and to buy some earrings. When all of a sudden lights and sirens came up behind them and they were pulled over by the police.

"Why did he stop us?" asks Markéta.

"I don't know why," says Vanessa.

"Do you have your insurance and registration stuff in here?" asks Markéta. She reaches into the glove box. The officer walks up and Vanessa lets her window down.

"Ma'am, your license and registration please."

"Was I speeding or something?" Vanessa gives the officer her license. He doesn't immediately answer her then he points toward the dark tint on her windows. Vanessa looks at Markéta as if to say, *can you believe this.* The officer then looks over at Markéta then back at Vanessa. "Is there anyone else in the car?" Vanessa just lets the window down so he can see for himself.

"Ma'am, can I look in your trunk?"

"Why do you need to look in my trunk?" Vanessa is now agitated. "No, you can't look in my trunk. You have no reason to look in my trunk."

"Ma'am, I'm going to have to ask you and your passenger to step out of the car."

The officer has them sit on the curb while two other squad cars were brought in. While they are sitting Markéta tells Vanessa, "I wouldn't have opened my trunk for him either. That's all they do is harass us anyway."

"Let me call my mom then you can call yours." Vanessa calls and tells her Mom what has happened, then hands the phone to Marketa who calls home, but nobody answers. DeMario was in the shower and Teresa was outside talking to Ms. Lillie, so she leaves a message on her mom's cell phone.

Shortly thereafter, Nicole picks up DeMario and they are headed to the game. "Do your parents know where I live?"

"No, why?" asks Nicole.

"Just wondering. They just let you roll like that?"

"My Mom is the one that asks all the questions. My dad is cool though. Would you like to meet them?" says Nicole. "We have time to stop by, but my dad may still be on the golf course."

"I don't know about that. Are you sure? I know they will ask a lot of questions about my family, school, and stuff."

"Trust me, it won't be that bad. Besides, my mom has been asking me about you. After you guys meet maybe she can stop asking me so many questions."

"Okay, let's get it out the way," says DeMario.

They make a detour towards the Air Force base where Nicole lives. They pass through the gates of the base and head toward the housing area. DeMario points out where his mom works as they pass the base lodging.

"I've only been on this base a few times even though my mom has worked here for a while."

"My mom likes living on base because people just can't drive by and bother you."

"I know what she means by that. We had a neighbor down the corner from us have someone shoot through their window two nights ago, and they have no idea who did it or why," says DeMario. As they are pulling into the driveway, Nicole's mom is taking groceries out of the car.

"I thought you were headed to the football game?" She notices DeMario and smiles. "Well, you must be DeMario?"

"Yes Ma'am, can I help you with that?" DeMario reaches for the grocery bag.

"Sure, if you like, one of those bags has charcoal in it. Nicole's father says he might barbecue tomorrow. I'll cross my fingers on that. He'll likely be back on the golf course." DeMario follows Nicole and her Mom into the house. The house is so neat and orderly, almost like they were expecting company.

"Is it always this clean?" he asked Nicole.

"You simply aren't looking hard enough."

"Well, it looks clean enough to me. You should see our house sometimes."

Once the groceries are put away, Nicole's mom comes back into the kitchen. "So, we finally get to meet. I was beginning to think you didn't exist." She looks at Nicole with a grin.

"Yes, ma'am," was all DeMario could think to say.

"Mom, where is the little brat?"

"The little brat, as you call him, Nicholas is over at the community center. As a matter of fact, can you go to get him before you go to the game?"

"You know he's not going to be ready and he's just going to pout."

"Yes, you are probably right about that. I'll go and get him."

"I guess all little brothers are the same," says DeMario.

"Do you have a little brother?"

"Yes, ma'am and two sisters."

"One of his sisters is a cheerleader at the school, mom," says Nicole with a smile.

"Oh really?" says Nicole's mom with a grin. She looks at Nicole knowing what that statement is all about.

"Yes ma'am. She couldn't wait till tonight," says DeMario.

"So, what are your interests? Nicole told me you play baseball and that you are an excellent student and that you have some scholarship offers."

"Yes, I do okay with my studies."

"That's wonderful. I wish there were more young black men like you. Stay out of trouble and don't get caught up in the system. Your mom must be so proud. Seems she raised a fine young man."

"Okay Mom, we have to go," says Nicole as she looks at her mom with a *you are embarrassing me* look.

"I can take a hint." They hear the garage door open.

"Well, you may as well meet my dad. At least he'll be less inclined to ask a lot of questions," says Nicole. She looks back at her mother with a playful smile.

"It was nice to meet you, ma'am."

"It was nice to finally meet you too." Nicole leads the way out the doorway and into the garage. Nicole introduces DeMario to her father.

"Dad, this is DeMario."

"I am glad to meet you, young man," as he shakes DeMario's hand.

"I'm pleased to meet you too, sir."

"That's a firm handshake. You know, a handshake tells a great deal about a man."

"I learned that from my uncle. He's in the military also."

"Dad, we have to go before the game starts," says Nicole.

"Okay. You guys be careful out there tonight," he says. "Perhaps one day we can play a round of golf. Have you ever played golf before?"

"No, sir," says DeMario.

"One day I'll have to take you."

"Okay, that's it. We have to go now. Later, Dad," says Nicole. She grabs DeMario's arm and pushes him toward her car.

"That wasn't too bad," says DeMario.

"I guess not, but if my mom would have had more time you may be singing a different tune. She would have gone on and on."

"They seem pretty cool."

"I guess so," says Nicole as she is backing down the driveway.

"So, you and your dad have a convertible?" says

DeMario, looking at Nicole's father corvette.

"That's why I wanted one."

Back at home, Teresa is across the street talking to Ms. Lillie when Mercedes and Carlos return with Marcus.

"Look what dad bought me, two new outfits," says Mercedes. "He also bought Carlos something too."

"He bought me that new video game I told you about," says Carlos.

"Okay, you guys go put that stuff in the house. It's almost time to go to the game."

Teresa turns to Marcus still sitting in the car. "Look, Marcus, I think it's fantastic what you are doing for Mercedes and also what you did for Carlos..." Marcus interrupts her before she can finish.

"Teresa, before you go there, I'm just doing my part in showing these kids that all brothers are not the same. Some of us are taking care of our children. Mercedes is my only child, so I'm going to do right by her."

"Look, you didn't let me finish talking," says Teresa.

"Teresa, I know you too well. I already know what you were about to say," says Marcus.

The kids come out of the house and get into her car. Teresa turns back to Marcus. "Marcus, you are alright, and I am glad that you are doing your part. By the way, are you going to the game tonight?"

"No, I have to finish a car tonight," says Marcus.

"Markéta is cheering tonight for the first time at a football game."

"Oh really, that's tonight?" says Marcus. "Wish I would have known a little earlier, but you know I don't keep up with these things anymore." The kids are in the car hollering at Teresa.

"Mom, it's time to go!"

"Look, we got to go."

"Okay," says Marcus. He backs out of the driveway, waving his hand out the window as he drives off down the street. Teresa heads toward her car.

"Mercedes, did you lock the doors?"

"Yes Ma'am. All the doors," says Mercedes, handing Teresa the keys.

"Are you guys ready to see big sis do her thing tonight?" says Teresa.

They drive to the football stadium. Once they find a parking space, they make their way toward the gate. Teresa looks at her cell phone and notices that she has a missed message. After she reads the message, she stops in her tracks.

"Are you kidding me?"

"What, Mama? What is it?" says Mercedes.

"Markéta and Vanessa are down at the city jail."

"Mama, why are they in jail?" says Mercedes in a frightened voice.

"Look, we have to go and find your brother. They should already be here," says Teresa.

"Mama, what's wrong? You are scaring me."

"Mercedes, baby, mama needs for you to calm down. Let me call Vanessa. Then we have to find your brother." Teresa hits redial on her phone. "Hello Vanessa, what is going on, let me speak to Markéta?"

Markéta tells Teresa about the situation and everything that had happened. "I'm about to come down there and act a fool, as soon as I find your brother to watch these kids." When they find DeMario and Nicole, Teresa tells him and the cheerleading coach about the situation.

By the time Teresa got to the police station, Vanessa's mother has already made it and is talking to the officer in charge.

"So, what is going on down here?" says Teresa.

"They wanted permission to look into the trunk of her car for no good reason but to harass these girls," says Vanessa mother.

Teresa turns around and asks the policeman, "Where is my daughter?"

"Ma'am, I've already explained it to this woman what happened," says the officer pointing to Vanessa's mom.

"There was a misunderstanding, but we've worked it out." That wasn't enough for Teresa.

"They shouldn't have been stopped in the first place. Is this all y'all do all day? Harass people, especially us..." By now, another police officer steps in.

"Ms. Dupart, as the officer stated, it was a mix-up. The car fit the description of a stolen vehicle."

"Man, I ain't buying that! Next, you going to tell me the girls fit the description too. Where are the girls?" says Teresa. The officer pointed behind her. The girls were there the whole time on the other side of the partition. Teresa turns back to the officers. "Tonight, my daughter was supposed to cheer at her first football game, and you guys just screwed that up." With that, Teresa turns to Vanessa's mom and the girls. "Let's go." And out the door, they go with the girls giggling behind them.

13

WHEN T H E Y A R R I V E back at the football game, it is almost half time. The girls go running up to take their place with the other cheerleaders. DeMario and Nicole are sitting with Mercedes and Carlos when Mercedes hollers, "There goes Markéta, I see her! I see her!"

"I see her too," says Carlos. DeMario and Nicole are now standing up looking for his mother.

"Do you see her yet?" asks Nicole.

"Not yet. With all these people standing up it's going to be hard to find her."

"She just found us, she's coming up," says Nicole, pointing to Teresa.

"Good, now we can go sit on the upper level," says DeMario.

"Mom, I see you got Markéta out of jail."

"That was bogus," says Teresa and a few more choice words which made Nicole laugh. Teresa had met Nicole once at the mall.

"I'll catch you guys at home," says DeMario.

"We'll be sitting closer to the cheerleaders so that I can see my baby girl," says Teresa.

After moving to a higher level and greeting some of their friends, DeMario and Nicole find a spot where they can take in the football field better. "I like to be near the top level so I can see the field better," says DeMario.

"I agree," says Nicole.

"Look at Big Mike," he says, pointing over at his

friend. "Still trying to talk to Monica Dell. He's been trying to talk to her ever since we were sophomores and she was a freshman, and she still pays him no mind. Her parents are very religious. I'm surprised she's at the game."

"That's her sister with her, Lorraine Dell. She's in my psychology class," says Nicole.

"I know Lorraine. We had a little puppy love thing back in eighth grade," says DeMario. Nicole narrows her eyes at him.

"Oh really?" says Nicole.

"Yeah, we speak from time to time, but that's about it," says DeMario. "I think Big Mike is color struck. All the girls he ever talks to are light skin and have what some people call good hair."

"I have good hair," says Nicole.

"You know what I mean. We used to go to the same church when my Grandmother was living. After she died, we stopped going."

"So, you guys don't go to church now?" asked Nicole.

"Very rarely. My mom doesn't make us go, and when we do, it's the church down the street on special occasions."

"There is no way I could get away with that at my house. My mom is a Sunday school teacher, so I have to go."

"It's not that she isn't religious. Ever since my Grandma died something just changed. Maybe losing her mom did it."

"Hey, maybe you can come to my church

59

sometimes," says Nicole.

"Maybe, we'll see," says DeMario.

Teresa and the children along with her co-worker Chantel and her son Tyson and Darlene's son Calvin were enjoying watching Markéta on the field. "Where is Darlene?"

"I believe I'm her default babysitter. She says the kids are great together. She doesn't think I know the difference," says Chantel. Teresa tells her about the police incident and how she handled it.

"Teresa, you are so crazy," says Chantel.

"If they thought my baby was going to miss her first game, they were so wrong. Those girls worked too hard for this night. Look at her out there doing the thing. You go, girl!"

"So, what did you do today?" asked Chantel.

"Something I shouldn't have done. I smoked one. Not just one, two."

"It must've been some good stuff. I hope you don't have to get tested no time soon on a random."

"I know, I just couldn't help myself, then Larry came over, and that was that," says Teresa.

"It probably was his fault," says Chantel.

"Not this time. I was already smoking one when he came over." They continued to talk, the game was almost over, so Markéta came over and asked her how good they were doing.

"Good, really good," says her mother. "I'm enjoying it."

"So, I can still go to Graffiti's with Vanessa?" she

asked.

"Yes, but don't be out past midnight. I need to get you a cellphone so that I can keep up with you. Here take mine and call me when you are on your way home," says Teresa as she hands Marketa her cellphone.

"Look and don't get arrested this time," says Chantel with a laugh.

"We won't," she said and ran off down the bleachers with her friends.

"That girl is going to be just like you."

"Hmm, she already is. I told her she stole my body." The game was coming to an end, and the home team was winning by two touchdowns. The stands began to empty as people were trying to beat the traffic.

Nicole asked DeMario, "Are you ready to go? We're winning, and we can beat some of the traffic."

"At this point, we may as well wait until it's over. By the time we get to the car the traffic will be long," says DeMario.

"Yeah, you're probably right," says Nicole. "Remember, I have to be home before midnight, so hopefully, we can get to Graffiti's and still have a decent parking spot."

"Yeah, after winning, tonight is going to be off the chain at ffiti's tonight," says DeMario. The two begin to walk down the aisle toward the car.

14

AFTER THEY FINALLY make their way to Graffiti's many of their friends are already there in a festive mood, eating, playing video games, dancing, and hanging out in the parking lot.

"Wow, you can barely move in this place," says Nicole. DeMario responds to her in a loud voice over the music playing.

"I know. Let's go to the other side of the room where the tables are."

While acknowledging their friends with gestures and hand motions, they make their way to the other side of the room. They find a table that needs to be cleaned off.

"By the time they get over here we could have done it ourselves," says DeMario, so they take a few napkins and clean off the table. "There is no way I could work here dealing with all these people."

"I'm sure it's not like this all the time. I think I would like it because you are staying busy and it would never be boring."

"I guess that's true, but still." Looking around the room, DeMario asks her, "Have you seen Vanessa or my sister yet?"

"No," replies Nicole. "Maybe they are outside, and we just didn't see them."

"Maybe you're right," says DeMario. He was looking around to see if he could find Marketa or the friends she hung with. He knew how easy it was for his sister to get caught up in some type of drama with some girl. Most of the guys knew he was her brother and that he was a protector of his sister. Besides, he could handle himself in a fight if need be.

Markéta and Vanessa have just arrived at Graffiti's and found a parking spot that someone had just vacated. "DeMario and Nicole are here. There's her car," says Vanessa, looking toward Nicole's beetle.

"Where?"

"Over there," says Vanessa. She points toward the car.

"I bet he's wondering where I am."

"For sure, you know he is." As they are heading up the ramp to go inside, there's a horn blowing. It's the twins Isaac and Isaiah.

"Hey, I see you made it," says Isaiah talking to Markéta. "I told you we were going to beat them boys. I know you saw that interception I got."

"Yeah, and I watched you drop one too," says Markéta, walking toward the car.

"Look, I'm going in while y'all talking," says Vanessa in air quotes. She turns and heads toward the inside of the building. Isaac tells her to hold up as he gets out of the car.

"Can't go in there with no girl by my side." With that, they both laughed and went into the building. As Isaiah gets out of the car, Markéta sits on the hood.

"Shorty, you better get off my hood."

"Make me?" says Markéta with a grin on her face.

15

BY NOW TERESA has made it back home and gotten her youngest two children off to bed. Chantel, Larry, Ms. Lillie and a few other neighbors have come over. They are all out back in the backyard playing cards, dominoes, and gambling, while also drinking and smoking marijuana. It's their usual Friday night ritual only this time, it's at her place. It's a BYOB party better known as bring your own bottle.

"So, Ms. Lillie, when am I going to see you with a man?" asks Chantel. Ms. Lillie had retired from working at the base. She was the reason Teresa was able to get a job there.

"I don't need no man, for what?" Then she continued. "Nooo lawd, why do I need some man lying around my house, eating up my food, don't want to work. I'm retired. What I need a man for? I got my own money and my own house."

They started laughing, mostly at the way she was expressing it.

"There's a difference in needing a man and *needing* a man," says Chantel. "If you catch my drift."

"We all get it," says Teresa while laughing and shaking her head in understanding.

"Well, I'm passed both of those stages," says Ms. Lillie.

Back at Graffiti's, DeMario and Nicole were now eating their food and mingling with some of the other students. DeMario spots his sister with Isaiah on the other side of an elevated platform enjoying the music and festivities along with some of the other cheerleaders and wannabes. This is what she lived for; it was cool though, he thought.

In some aspects he understood it, no one wanted to be an outcast, especially with girls. He knew how horrible they could sometimes be toward one another and how easy their feelings could be hurt, mainly from other girls.

"Hey man, why aren't you playing ball this year?" It was Melvin one of his friends who graduated a year early. "What's up, Mel? I'm concentrating on those studies, but I am going to play baseball. What have you been up to?"

"Man, I'm just in town for the weekend. I came home to see my mom. She's sick, you know."

"Aw man, I didn't know that," says DeMario. "So, how's your Pops?"

"Man, you know Pops, he's still working, but if something happens to Mom, I don't know what he's going to do. I'm gone, my two sisters are gone, you know, my dad never learned to cook outside of barbecuing," says Melvin with a laugh.

16

BACK AT HOME, things have begun to get a little unsettling. Two of the men playing cards, Jessie and Bubba Wayne, have gotten drunk and high. They are arguing about one of them cheating. Jessie, the youngest and the larger of the two, was claiming Bubba Wayne was cheating him. The two of them had never gotten along. One was always bad mouthing the other, both of them had criminal records and been in jail multiple times.

"You must think I'm dumb," says Jessie.

"Look, boy, get yo young tail up if you can't play with the big boys. Y'all get this young punk out my face," says Bubba Wayne.

By now Jessie had stood up and reached over the table and hit Bubba Wayne in the jaw. He was about to hit him again when Bubba Wayne reached into his jacket and before Jessie had a chance to react Bubba Wayne had pulled a knife out and stabbed him twice, once in his stomach and once in the chest. Jessie grabbed his chest, stunned, his eyes wide, then he cried out, "Man, you stabbed me," as he fell across the table.

"I told you bout messing wit me. Now look at you, bleeding all over the place."

Everybody was screaming and hollering. Jessie tried to get up from the table and fell back down in the chair with blood all over his clothes.

"Call the ambulance, somebody please, please, please!" says Ms. Lillie. Teresa had already run in the house calling 911.

"Hey man, don't try to get up!" says Larry.

Jessie tried to get up again. One last time, he fell back with his eyes open, but Jessie would never see again.

"I told y'all! I told y'all! This was going to happen one day. Those two were going to kill one another," says Ms. Lillie.

Bubba Wayne never even tried to run. He went around the front yard sat on the porch lit a cigarette and waited for the police to arrive. With all the commotion going on Carlos and Mercedes were now up. By the time the emergency services got to their home, they were already aware of what had occurred. Teresa told them to stay in their rooms, all the time trying to contact Markéta but couldn't get an answer.

Teresa, along with several of the guests, was being questioned by the police after they arrested Bubba Wayne.

The phone rang. It was Markéta. "Hey Mom, I missed your call."

"Markéta, where are you?"

"I'm at Graffiti. I told you where we were going," says Markéta.

"Markéta, listen to me. Something has happened over here. Bubba Wayne just killed Jessie on the back porch."

"What!"

"Get your brother and y'all come on home, you hear me?"

"Yes, ma'am." After hanging up. Markéta tells Isaiah

what had just happened. They start looking for DeMario and Nicole. Once Markéta spots DeMario she waved him over and told him what has just happened.

"Are you kidding me? I knew it, I knew it! All those crazy people," says DeMario. The word must be getting around about what has happened because kids are looking at both him and Markéta. Nicole says she would take them both home. Everyone is pretty much silent during the drive. They can see the police lights as they get closer. The road on both ends is blocked off. Most of the neighbors are standing outside. DeMario tells Nicole to let them out and that he will call her tomorrow. They can see one of the local news crews has made their way to the scene with one of the reporters talking to some of the neighbors. As DeMario and his sister approach the house, an officer attempts to prevent them from coming onto the lawn until DeMario tells him they live there. They could see their mother out back with an officer, so DeMario goes to the rear of the house to check on his younger siblings. They were in their mom's room watching TV.

"D, we saw a dead man tonight," says Carlos.

"No, we didn't. He was under a sheet," says Mercedes.

"Were you guys afraid?" says Markéta.

"No, I was asleep. Then I heard all that noise," says Carlos.

DeMario sat with his sisters and brother until their mother came into the room. "Are they all gone now, Momma?" says Mercedes.

"No, there are a few of them outside, talking with some of the other people," says Teresa with a sigh, looking at her two oldest as if she was waiting for them to say something.

"So, neither one of you guys has anything to say?"

Both DeMario and Marketa looked at one another. "Mama, what do you expect us to say?" says DeMario.

"I can't control what grown people do. If I had known how bad it was between those two, I wouldn't have let one of them come over."

"Mom, is their blood on the porch?" says Mercedes. "We saw blood on that sheet. I don't want to go out there anymore."

"Come to Mama," says Teresa. She reaches out her hands to Mercedes and gives her a hug. DeMario gets up. "Where are you going?"

"To clean up the porch," he states.

"You don't have to do that. I'll do it tomorrow morning."

"Mom, I got it," says DeMario, as he walks out the room. He waited nearly two hours until all the police were gone and the streets were quiet again. DeMario gathers the cleaning supplies and goes out on the back porch. He takes the chair Jessie was sitting in and dumps it into the trash can. He then sprays down the porch with cleaning supplies. As he is cleaning Teresa comes out of the house.

"Is it coming up?" she asks.

"Yeah, most of it. I had to go over it several times in some spots, but it's coming up. What happen?"

"Jessie says Bubba Wayne was cheating. Who knows? They both were probably cheating."

"Mercedes says she doesn't want to come out here anymore."

"She just scared right now. I think she will be okay in a few days," says Teresa. "I hate this had to happen D, you know that, right?"

"Yes ma'am, I know that," says DeMario. He was about to say something else when the phone rang.

"Mama, telephone, it's Uncle Nate," says Markéta.

Teresa had tried to call him to let him know what had happened, but he wasn't available, so she left a message on his phone. Teresa took the phone and went into the yard talking to her brother. DeMario could hear some of what was being said. He could tell from the tone of his mother's voice how upset she was. She paced back and forth in the yard, smoking a cigarette while she was still on the phone with his uncle. After talking on the phone for a while, Teresa gives DeMario the telephone. "Here, Nate wants to speak to you."

"How are you holding up, man?"

"I'm doing okay. The others are a little shaken up," says DeMario.

"You know, I knew those fellas. Jessie beat up someone with a bat before, beat him senseless. I guess size doesn't always matter, but another case of brothers killing each other. One day we are going to learn, I hope."

"I can't wait to leave here," says DeMario.

"I understand you, but don't be in such a hurry to leave, young blood. The world out here is no joke either."

"I know what you're saying is right, but having someone killed on your back porch ... even you have to agree that's just crazy, Uncle Nate."

"I can't dispute any of that, but look, you guys are still together. Your mom knows that what happened tonight shouldn't have happened, and she regrets that it did. That's another reason not to be in such a hurry to leave. She needs your help with your brother and sisters as much as possible. What about that job your mom says you got?"

"What job?"

"She said you got a call from a sandwich shop saying you got the job."

"She didn't tell me that. I guess with all that went on tonight, she hasn't had time to tell me or she forgot."

"Perhaps. As you know I'll be coming down for Christmas," says Uncle Nate.

"Guess I'll see you then," says DeMario.

"Okay, see you then."

Teresa called Aunt Janice and talked to her for a while after everyone had gone to bed, and things calmed down. Afterward, she lay across her bed reflecting on the day's events. She was never one to show much fear, but somehow tonight was different. She felt a cold sweat come over her almost as if she was waiting for a verdict of some sort. While she lay there thinking, she turns over and looks at a picture of herself, with her mother, father, and Nate from many years ago. Their father had abandoned them a long time ago, and no one knew if he was dead or alive.

Tears begin to form in her eyes. *Mom, where are you*

now when I need you, she thought. Teresa felt herself shaking uncontrollably. Her mom had been dead now for almost six years from complications of diabetes. She always had them in church, even when Teresa had her kids, her mom would see to it that they went to church as much as possible.

Teresa hadn't read the Bible much since her mother passed and she only made the kids go to church on special holidays. Why should she go to church, she thought? Her mother always read her Bible and went to church, but it didn't save her from her condition. Even as she thought it, somehow, she didn't really believe it. It was just easier to think that way. Usually, at a time like this, she would just get another drink or get her smokes. Teresa sat up in her bed, turned on her bed lamp while catching a reflection of herself in the mirror. She looked tired and worn out. Maybe all the drinking, smoking, and to add to that all the *stress* was slowly wearing her down. She was still in her thirties and yet she felt as though she had already lived a full life.

Reflecting on her life, she thought about the last night she saw Mario, the father of DeMario and Markéta. They had just come from the club when he dropped her off at her Mom's house. They were supposed to have stopped to get some pampers and milk before they went home, but they had forgotten to do so. He dropped her off. That was the last time she saw him alive. After dropping Teresa off, Mario picked up one of his friends. While they were leaving the store, they got into an argument with some drug dealers on the corner about his friends' drug deals. Shots were fired and Mario was killed. Sometimes she just wondered what life would be like if he was still around. He was always there for his kids, even though her mother always blamed him for getting her pregnant.

Teresa knew the real reason her mother didn't like him. It was because he was older than her and he hadn't finished school which made her mother think there was no future with him. Nate didn't like him for some of the same reasons and because he thought Mario started dating Teresa because they had once dated the same girl and that was Mario's way of getting back at him. Teresa didn't know about this until later; she always thought it was funny. Finally, she dozes off to sleep.

17

THE FOLLOWING MORNING no one was eager to get up. Everyone stayed in bed until finally, DeMario got up and knocked on his mom's door. "Come in."

"Hey, Mom you up yet?"

"Depends on your definition of up," she stated.

"I just want to know how you are," he says. "And about that sub shop job. Uncle Nate says you told him I got the job."

"Oh yeah. They called yesterday and said to come by Monday."

"Cool. I was beginning to wonder was I going to get it," says DeMario, sitting on his mom's bed.
Right about that time they heard raindrops on the roof.

"You know, sometimes when it rains, I just want to stay in bed all day," says Teresa. "When I was a little girl, Nate and I would go outside to play in the rain. My momma would be saying 'get out of that rain!', especially me, because she knew I hated getting my hair done."

Teresa picked up a photo album and looked through the pictures with DeMario. "Look at you graduating from the sixth grade."

"Yeah, the sixth grade. Why do they have graduation for the sixth grade?"

"That's because it was your last year at that school."

"I still find it ... what's the word I'm looking for?"

"Stupid?" says Teresa.

"Yes, that's the word I'm looking for, stupid," says

DeMario.

"I figured that was the word you were looking for." The rain was coming down harder now, and the wind began to blow. DeMario looked out the window.

"Perhaps the rain can wash out the remainder of the bloodstains on the porch."

"True, but it won't wipe away the memories from last night," says Teresa. "I still can't believe what happened last night. I've seen many things D, but I've never seen anyone get killed with my own eyes. I once witnessed a dead man in the alley, an old wino. We just believed he was drunk until it was revealed the following day that he passed away a day or so earlier but nothing like last night."

"Mom, you ever think about moving from here?"

"I always think about moving from here. Thinking about it and doing it are two different things. It's not that easy," says Teresa. "You think most of the people that live here want to be here?"

"Probably not, but some of them don't seem to care. I mean, look at how some of them act," says DeMario.

"Where you live shouldn't determine your behavior," says Teresa. Marketa then comes into the room and joins him on their mother's bed.

"Hey girlie girl, how you doing this morning?" says Teresa to Marketa.

"I'm getting along fine. It feels like I slept all morning, now I'm hungry."

"Yeah, we all had a long night," says Teresa. "There's some breakfast food in there, sausage, grits, and eggs."

"Mom, what are you going to cook today?" uttered Marketa. "I got a taste for some Frogmore stew."

"With or without potatoes?" says Teresa.

"With, of course," says Marketa.

"What about breakfast?" says DeMario. Carlos and Mercedes have made their way to Teresa's room as well.

"I want some cereal," says Carlos. "Do we have any milk? Someone needs to go and buy some milk."

"D, go and buy some milk, and bring back some potatoes too," says his mother.

"I'll cook the breakfast," offered Marketa.

"Let me wash up first," says DeMario.

"I'm hungry *now*," says Carlos.

"You can always eat it with water," says DeMario with a grin on his face. Carlos makes a disgusted face, and the family laugh. After DeMario gets cleaned up, he takes his mom's car to the grocery store. As he is getting the items, he noticed the morning paper mentions last night's killing. DeMario buys a copy of the newspaper. Once he gets home, he keeps the paper to himself and goes to his room.

The article gives some details about what happened and also gives their address. The writer says that this kind of thing happens a lot in this neighborhood. The article also says that it may have been gang-related, which made DeMario angry. There weren't any gangs in his neighborhood, just hustlers. He didn't like living in his neighborhood, but he didn't like an outsider lying about it either, especially for publicity. The phone rings. It was Nicole.

"Hello, just phoned to check on you guys," says Nicole.

"I'm doing okay, I guess. Just sitting here reading the paper about last night and the lies they are telling," says DeMario. "What happened last night had nothing to do with gang violence. Anyhow, that job I applied for at the sandwich shop, I got it."

"Oh yeah? That's great," says Nicole.

Carlos knocked on the door. "Breakfast is ready."

"I'll be there in a minute," says DeMario. "Hey, what are you doing later?"

"I'm not sure. It's supposed to rain all day today," says Nicole.

"Yeah, it's raining hard over here too. Well, I guess I'll see you Monday."

"Okay, bye," says Nicole. DeMario makes his way toward the kitchen where everyone else is already eating.

"I hate the thunder and lightning," says Carlos.

"That's because you are so bad and now you are afraid," says Mercedes.

"Don't say that," says Markéta.

"I'm sure she's just kidding," says Teresa.

"I'm just saying," says Mercedes.

"I'm thinking about going to church tomorrow since we haven't been in a while," says Teresa as she looks at her children.

"Ooh wee, I want to go to church tomorrow," says Mercedes.

"Which church are you talking about, the one down

the street or the one that Grandma used to belong to?" says Marketa.

"I'm thinking about going to the one grandma used to go to, the one I grew up in," says Teresa. "I still know a lot of people that still go to that church. I still have some friends there."

"After what happened last night, maybe going to church is a good thing," says Marketa. "I can put on my cute little outfit."

"See, you don't just go to church to look good. You are already going for the wrong reason," says DeMario.

"I can wear a cute outfit!" she sounds off. "What's wrong with that?"

"Which outfit would that be?" remarked DeMario. "I hope not the one you had on the first day of school."

"DeMario, leave your sister alone. I'm sure she knows what to wear to church and what not to wear," says Teresa.

"Mr. Negative always has something to say, but if I was going to wear that outfit, it's my business," says Marketa with a scowl on her face.

"You two need to cut it out," says Teresa pointing at the both of them.

"Hey Mom, are you going to Jessie's funeral?" asked DeMario.

"D, I haven't even thought about it," says Teresa with a sigh.

"Why would you ask her that? That's a stupid question to ask. The man just died last night! Give her some room to breathe," says Markéta with her hand's half way in the air.

DeMario knew Markéta was right. It was too soon to ask his mother about a funeral. What a stupid question. He should have known better. After everyone had finished eating breakfast and did their chores, everyone went into their rooms.

It was still thundering and lightning outside, and the rain was coming down hard. Teresa was going over some school work that she had been working on trying to finish it up; it was hard for her to concentrate with so many things going on in her mind. Her cell phone rang, making it even more impossible to concentrate. It was Marcus on the other end.

"I heard about what happened last night, is everybody okay?"

"Hey Marcus, yes everybody is managing all right, thanks for asking."

"Do you need anything? You want me to come by and pick up the kids or something?" says Marcus.

"No, not in this rain, but thanks. Marcus, you are a good man," says Teresa.

"I've been trying to get you to see that for a long time now," says Marcus laughing.

"I guess I asked for that, you got me," says Teresa laughing.

"Hey, I have a car that the owner never picked up, it's a Honda Civic. It's in fairly good condition. I had to fix the transmission on it. I can sell it to DeMario---" he paused.

"For $400, he can pay me $50 a month. What do you think about that?"

"Marcus, are you sure? He just got a part-time job. He's been wanting a car for a long time. With his new job he can pay for the insurance."

"The insurance on it shouldn't be that much because of the age of the car, and it's a good running car and good on gas."

"That boy is going to be excited about having his own car. Marcus, you know I hate people to be all in my business, but in this case, how can I say no? The boy does need a car to get around, and it takes a load off me having to take off sometimes to take them everywhere."

"Hey, look, Teresa, you don't have to explain to me. I know you, that's what always drew me to you in the first place," says Marcus. "I know you are headstrong, independent, don't need nobody."

"Stop right there, I don't need a history lesson," says Teresa. "I get your point."

"No, I can go on," says Marcus.

"No, you already said enough. So, Marcus, why haven't I seen you with a lady friend yet?"

"Because I'm waiting for the right one," says Marcus. "They say patience is a virtue, and I'm waiting as long as it takes."

"You don't want to wait too long; you may lose out on something good."

"What's the rush? I have my own business. I have a beautiful daughter and check this out, I get along well with her mother," says Marcus.

"You are too funny, you need to quit," says Teresa. "When will DeMario be able to get the car?"

"He can get it next week. Let me finish up a few things on it," says Marcus. "As a matter of fact, he can come by and help me finish it up."

"Thanks again, Marcus. I'll tell him about it," says Teresa.

"No problem. With all those cars I have out back, I need to get rid of some of them. I need the space," says Marcus. "Hey, I'm getting another call. I'll see you guys later."

"Alright, bye," says Teresa. After she hangs up the telephone, Teresa finishes up with her paperwork, then heads toward the kitchen to begin cooking the Frogmore stew. Teresa makes the meal thinking about how happy DeMario is going to be once he knows about the car from Marcus. DeMario always liked Marcus so there shouldn't be any issues about accepting the car from him.

Rain is still coming down hard the entire time she's making the meal. *It seems no one is going anywhere today,* she thought, which was all right with her.

"I think we should all watch a movie together," says Marketa. "It's my turn to choose."

"I don't want to see a movie. I just want to play my games," says Carlos.

"What type of movie? Let me guess a chick flick?" says DeMario.

"My turn, my choice," says Marketa.

81

"You know guys, I do think we should all watch a movie, including you Carlos, but I believe that it should be a good family movie, and we can watch it in my room," says Teresa.

"Mom, I think I like that idea better," says Markéta. After eating their meal, they pile into Teresa's room to get ready to watch the movie.

"What's this movie about?" whined Carlos.

"It's a movie about some kids who lost their parents at the mall," says Markéta. "I saw it over Vanessa's house. It's good and funny."

Everyone settles on the bed while Markéta puts on the movie. Once the movie is finished, everyone seems to have enjoyed it.

"That was a good movie," says Teresa. "Wouldn't you agree, Carlos?"

"It was a good movie. Can we see it again?" says Carlos.

"Maybe tomorrow night," says Teresa "Make sure you guys get your clothes ready tonight, especially you Markéta. I don't want to be late for church tomorrow morning. We are going to the early morning service."

Afterward, Teresa put away the food. She then closed the blinds. The rain had slowed to a sprinkle. It was at that point that it occurred to her that she hadn't smoked a cigarette all day.

18

THE FOLLOWING MORNING the sunlight is shining bright, everyone is up on time, and ready to get to church.

"Does anyone have a Bible beside me?" asks Teresa.

"I have one grandma gave me," revealed DeMario.

"Okay, anyone else? I have a small one in the car," says Teresa.

"I have one somewhere," mumbled Markéta.

"It's time to go, everyone in the car. D, make sure everything is turned off and locked up," says Teresa as she heads out the door and into the car.

"Let's go, Markéta you had last night and this morning to get ready," says DeMario.

"I'm ready, I was just looking for that Bible," says Markéta.

"Too late to find it now, it's time to go, mom is already in the car."

"All right," says Markéta with her eyes rolling.

On the drive to church, Teresa tells them that she wants them all to sit together and tells Mercedes and Carlos no talking in the church. Once they are all seated in the church, Teresa casually observes some of the people that still attend the service. After all these years, she still remembers some of the older people and a few her age. There are also a lot of new faces. Some she knew from the neighborhood and other places. The new pastor wasn't much older than her. She remembered when he used to lead the choir.

DeMario was enjoying the service, especially the

83

parts where the young people were involved. They seem to be enjoying what they were doing. He had never actually put much thought into religion. Even as a child going to church with his grandmother, it was just church. While observing the young people, he knew from school sing and worship it gave him a better understanding of why some of them behaved differently than he and some of the others at school.

Most kids his age would rather sit in the back and count down the time until the service is over. He even enjoyed the sermon given by a young woman telling about all the things she had gone through in her life and how God had spared her from a bad relationship. Listening to her speak was having an effect on DeMario. Some of the things she was saying brought back memories of his grandmother. Some were the same things she used to tell them about God and Jesus.

After the service was over, the pastor and his wife greeted some of the people. The pastor stopped them as they were about to leave. "Sister Dupart! How long has it been?" says the pastor, shaking her hand. "It's been a while since I've seen you and the kids."

"Yes, it has Pastor. The last time I was here, you were the assistant pastor."

"Has it been that long?" says his wife. "My, your kids have grown up."

"Yes, they sure have," replied Teresa rubbing the top of Carlos' head.

"Hopefully, we'll be seeing you guys again real soon. God bless," says the pastor. "We sure do miss your mother."

"Thank you for your kind words," says Teresa.

Other people greeted them once they were outside of the church. On their way home in the car, Markéta says, "Mom, I think that preacher held your hand too long."

"Markéta! Don't say that!" says Teresa with a laugh. She asks them if they enjoyed the service. They all say yes. That's when she told DeMario about the car that Marcus was selling him.

"What, he's getting a car?" says Markéta. "Tell Marcus to give me one too."

"He's not giving it to him Markéta." DeMario was so happy Teresa had to tell him to slow down because he was driving them home.

"See Mom, I told you Marcus is a cool dude," says DeMario.

"He told me he had a surprise for you. He said not to tell anyone," says Mercedes with a smile on her face.

The rest of the afternoon was a restless one for DeMario. From the church services to having his own car. He had to tell Nicole, so he video called her on his laptop to tell her the good news.

"Can you imagine getting a car and a job in the same week?" says DeMario.

"Wow, that's fantastic news, so when do you pick up the car?"

"I think I can pick it up sometime this week. I guess whenever I go over there to get it. Maybe you can take me over there to get it," says DeMario.

"With a car now, you can come and pick me up sometimes. I know you'd prefer that anyway," says Nicole laughing. "How was the church service? Did you enjoy it?"

"You know I enjoyed it, especially the parts where the young people were involved. I didn't know that Lorraine and Monica Dell could sing like that."

"Oh yes, Monica is really talented. She sings in the school choir," says Nicole. "So, did you speak to Lorraine?"

"No, why did you ask?" says DeMario. "I told you that was puppy love."

"I know, I was just kidding with you," says Nicole. "Sometimes I play the piano for our youth department when the regular musician isn't there."

"I always wished I could play guitar. My mom has Mercedes taking piano lessons from Ms. Lillie since she's always messing with it every time she's over there," says DeMario. As he was talking, Carlos comes into the room and was making funny faces at the camera.

"Guess it's time for me to go. I'll see you tomorrow," says DeMario.

19

ALL DAY MONDAY, DeMario's mind wasn't entirely focused on his class work. He was thinking about the car. He told Big Mike about it while they were riding home on the bus.

"Man, we are going to be rolling now! Going to all the games, parties, everything," says Big Mike. "I can help you with the gas. I'm tired of my sister taking me places." While Big Mike was talking. DeMario mind was already thinking about the things he can do with his own car and the independence it would give him.

The following day after school is finally over. Nicole drives DeMario over to Marcus garage to pick up his car with $75 as a down payment. Marcus tells him to keep the $75 and just start paying him the following month.

"Keep that money and use it for whatever you need for the car. It can help on some gas or something, and the car needs a good detail job on it," says Marcus.

"I can clean it myself. I wash my mom's car," says DeMario.

"It has a decent system in it already," say's Marcus. "Just get you some better speakers."

"I'm not concerned about that right now. I'm simply glad to be drifting in my own car," says DeMario.

"Say what?" snapped Marcus.

"I'm joking, of course," laughed DeMario. Marcus hands him the keys.

"Thanks again Marcus, but I have to get to work at

my new job."

"Alright my man, just sign this paper and drive careful out there, and don't do anything stupid, but we already know you know better than that."

DeMario says goodbye to Nicole, telling her that he'll call her later. DeMario smiles as he's sitting behind the wheel of his new car. When he's driving to work all he can think of is, *now his car will be parked in the student parking lot at school, yes indeed.*

20

THE FOLLOWING WEEKS were mostly normal for Teresa and her family. The Sundays that Teresa didn't have to go to work, they went to church. DeMario was enjoying his car and his job at the sandwich shop. With his first check, he bought a cell phone. He was also getting a few more scholarship offers. He even got one from the Naval Academy.

At school Nicole, Lorraine, and two other girls were in the running for homecoming queen. Nicole didn't know she was in the running until the names came out. She asked DeMario who he had voted for. He just rubbed is chin as if he were thinking, which of course answered her question. Markéta made the Homecoming court for the juniors.

A week later, after the final votes were in, Lorraine won by a small margin over Nicole.

"I think my mom was more excited about it than I was. I'm glad for Lorraine; she's beautiful and smart."

"Somehow, I knew you would feel that way," replied DeMario. "Well, at least you won't have to worry about getting a dress and all that stuff."

"They still want me to participate as royalty."

"Cool. Markéta was talking about it last night at home. Going on about her gown, asking mom how should she do her hair."

"That sounds like her," says Nicole. "Have you narrowed your schools down yet?"

With a sigh, DeMario says, "It was three, then I got

that Naval Academy letter. I like Stedman University, Stiles and one of the HBCU schools."

"My dad would love it if I went to an HBCU. He has all his fraternity plaques and HBCU posters all over his so-called man cave."

"I'll call you tonight. I have to get to work. I'm closing the store this evening and I want to get an early start on the restocking."

"I should have applied for that job too."

"They only hired one person," says DeMario as he gets into his car. "Are you going home?"

"No, I have to stay here. We start the Homecoming practice in a few minutes."

"Oh yeah, that's right. My sister is all charged up about that. She lives for stuff like that."

21

TERESA AND CHANTEL finished up the last two adjoining rooms when Chantel mentioned she hadn't seen Teresa smoke a cigarette in a spell. "You know; I don't think I've smoked one since the night Bubba Wayne killed Jessie," she says with her hands on her hip as if she was thinking.

"Not even a joint?" asks Chantel.

"Nope, after that night I was no longer feeling it the way I used to."

"I guess that situation did something to you, huh?"

"Maybe so. The desire to do it is no longer there, at least at this point."

"I'm sure your kids are cool with that."

"They haven't said anything to me about it," acknowledged Teresa. "Maybe they haven't noticed, with so much going on in their lives. DeMario is doing his thing, Marketa with her cheerleading and now preparing for homecoming, Mercedes has piano lessons with Ms. Lillie, and Carlos doing whatever little boys do. He wanted to be in the Cub Scouts I just don't have the time."

After they were all done cleaning and putting their things away, Teresa was thinking about the conversation she had with Chantel on her way home. Was she making a change in her life subconsciously without knowing it? Certainly, there are things in her life she hadn't changed.

22

A F T E R S H E H A D gotten home and called Mercedes and Carlos from over Ms. Lillie's house, she gets the mail from the mailbox only to notice a letter from someone named Olivia Dupart from Texas. The only other Dupart Teresa knew was her brother Nate. It was their father's last name.

All her kids had their own father's last names. Reading the letter brought a frightening chill to her bones. The individual who composed the letter claimed she was the daughter of Steven Nathaniel Dupart. He was trying to reconnect with his children. The letter goes on to allege that she attempted to locate Teresa by phone but was unable to get a phone number for her. She, however, was able to obtain her address by utilizing the Internet. Teresa's home phone wasn't listed. The letter also stated that their father was alive and has heart disease. While reading the letter, Teresa remembered that her father was from somewhere in Texas.

Why? After all these years without him in her life. Just as she was about to make some changes, *he* shows up. The more she read, the more she became enraged. The writer goes on to say that she was reasonably sure she had the right Dupart after letting her father see some of the pictures Markéta had posted online. In the letter, Olivia says she only recently found out that she had a half-brother and sister. Teresa had to stop reading the letter. She hadn't seen her father since she was about four years old. A span of 30 something years. Her parents were common law married.

She put the letter away to start dinner all the while her mind was going around in circles. What should she do with this information? She would have to tell her brother Nate.

By the time dinner was ready, Markéta was home, eagerly going over the events of the day. Teresa was mostly nodding her head in agreement with what Markéta was saying. She just wasn't all there.

After helping her two youngest children with their homework, Teresa finishes reading the letter. All of Olivia and her father's contact information were inside it as well.

The rest of the night and all the next day while she was at work Teresa had that letter on her mind until finally, she decided to call her brother and tell him about the letter. When everyone was in their rooms, she went outside in the backyard to call him. "Hello, are you busy?"

"Not really, I'm out and about. What's up, everything okay?"

"Depends on what your version of okay is. I got a letter in the mail on yesterday from Texas from a person name Olivia Dupart and," she hesitated. "She says she's our half-sister. She lives with our dad who, get this, is married to her mother."

"What? Teresa don't play with me." Teresa goes into detail about everything included in the letter. "Are you serious? So, he has heart disease and now he wants to see us after all these years?" Teresa could hear it in her brother's voice that he was angry and upset. "I don't want to see him," protested Nate.

"Nate, I thought the same thing. What would I want

93

from him? She says she didn't know he had any other children until recently."

"Guess we can't get sore at her. Can you imagine if Mama was still alive?" reckoned Nate. "I remember she was hurt for a long time."

"She's going to want some response. What do you think I should tell her?" Just then, DeMario comes outside to let her know that he's home from work.

"Mama, why are you out here? Is everything okay?"

"I'm on the telephone with your Uncle Nate."

"Oh, tell him I said what's up. He's still coming for Christmas, right?"

"Yes, he's still coming. I'll be in the house in a few minutes."

"I don't know, Teresa, I just don't know. I wonder what he is expecting from us. We've made it this long without him."

Teresa surmised. "Do you think I should call her?"

"Call her and say what? I'm happy you found us?"

"Nate, I believe I should tell her something. She did take the time to find us."

"Teresa, that is up to you. I don't need the man. I told you, I don't want to see him. I remember a little more than you. He not only left Mama with all those medical bills to pay; the day he left, he was supposed to take her to the hospital for her medicine. He never showed up," Nate paused. "So, he left us and moved back to Texas."

Listening to her brother, Teresa could tell he was still angry with their father, significantly more so than she.

Perhaps that was because he was older and had more memories.

"I'll think about it, then I'll let you know. I haven't told the kids yet. I'll tell them tonight."

"Just keep me informed either way."

"I'll let you know. Hey, and don't forget to put that $350 in my account for Markéta's dress," says Teresa.

"I already took care of that."

"I hadn't checked it today," she remarked. "Thanks." After hanging up with her brother, Teresa returns to the house where DeMario is eating his supper. Markéta comes into the dining room.

"You usually eat at the shop," she says to DeMario. "I have something to tell you guys."

"What, Mom?" says Markéta. "Is there something wrong?"

"You are always talking about me being cynical look at you," DeMario sounds off.

"First of all, I would never say cynical and second, shut up," insisted Markéta turning to her mother. "What is it, Mama?"

"Behave," says Teresa. "I got some information about my Dad on yesterday."

"What, is he dead or something? What?"

"Slow down, girl," Teresa insisted. "Are you going to let me finish?"

"Yeah, Markéta, let her finish."

DeMario and Markéta were in shock as Teresa told them about the letter. The three of them sat around the table talking about it.

"That was what you and Uncle Nate was talking about on the phone? What did he say about it?"

"He's upset, perhaps more than I am. I was younger than he was when our Dad left."

"Are you going to go and see him?" asks DeMario.

"I don't know yet. I haven't decided one way or the other."

"Are you going to call her?"

"I haven't decided that either."

"I think I would be mad about it," says Markéta. "I mean, what if he hadn't gotten heart disease? Would he have tried to communicate with you guys? I'm just saying."

"Mama, was it him or his daughter that tried to reach you guys?" asks DeMario.

"I think once he told her that he had two other children, that's what started this whole thing." She paused as if she was thinking out loud. "I wonder what her mother thinks about it. Anyway, it's time to go to bed."

The three of them cleaned up the kitchen. Afterward, DeMario and Markéta went to bed. Teresa stayed up to finish up some class work, still wondering what should she do. Should she be happy knowing that her father was still alive, or should she be angry with him? If this had been any other time in her life, she wouldn't have cared to see her father no matter the situation, especially the way he left them. Was it possible, her going to church was having an impact on her thinking.

23

THE NEXT DAY after getting everyone off to school, Teresa decides to give Olivia a call, but first, she texts Nate to let him know of her plans. He told her it was up to her if that's what she wanted to do. After reading the letter once again, she gathers her thoughts, then she called Olivia.

"Hello, may I speak to Olivia?"

"This is she."

"Hi, I'm Teresa Dupart."

"Hello, how are you? I realize contacting you out of the blue may not have been such a good idea, but after learning about you and your brother, I felt it was my duty to find you. I realize I may be opening up some old wounds." There was a paused from Olivia as if she wanted Teresa to respond to her.

"Olivia, I hadn't thought a great deal about my father in a long time, and neither has my brother. I have my life, and he chose his. He decided to leave us, that was his decision. He never once tried to find out how we were doing. I don't know what was going on between him and my mother, but I do know this, he left her when she was sick with his two kids. Those are the facts."

"Teresa, I can't begin to understand your pain, so I won't try. I can only hope that you can see that he is now reaching out."

As the conversation continued, Teresa learned that her father, who was part Creole, returned home and married a Creole woman. He had been working on the railroad from the time he left them and moved back to his hometown near Beaumont, Texas. Teresa asks her how her mother felt about it once she learned he had a family before them.

"She asks him a lot of questions. I don't think she was angry or anything, probably because of his present condition. He's at the hospital now with my mom." She asks Teresa if she wanted to speak to him once he was back home. Teresa had to think about it for a moment.

"Maybe at a later date, but not right now. And if I speak to him, I think I want it to be in person."

"I understand. I would feel the same way," says Olivia.

The longer Teresa talked to Olivia, the more she felt at ease with her. She told her about her situation, about her children, and her line of work.

"Sounds like you have your hands full."

"With two children in high school, one who will graduate this coming year and the other one Marketa think she's grown already ... Yes, I have my hands full, but they are good kids."

"I see her photos on her profile online. I just love her hair."

"Oh, my goodness her hair," Teresa exclaimed. "I told her it would grow longer if she let me cut it; she almost cried. I'm thinking about going back natural myself. I haven't made up my mind yet. I don't do wigs. The idea of giving other people all that money, no, that's what my momma taught me, so I'm natural a lot of the time." As they were talking Teresa gets a text from Larry asking if he can come over. She just ignored the text and continued speaking with Olivia.

Teresa then asks her some questions about herself. She found out that Olivia was in her junior year of college and afterward was going to MED school in Houston to become a heart specialist.

"Oh my, this is too real, I'm taking classes on health information management online to get my degree, I haven't told anyone not even my kids. They think I'm doing all this paperwork for my job. A friend of mine does it at the health department. I asked her some questions about it and that's how I got started. I don't want to be a housekeeper, all my life."

"That's wonderful! If you ever need any help, just let me know."

"Okay, I'm sure I'll run into a few problems with the medical classes. From what I heard others say at least. The rest I can handle."

"There are some classes that will be more challenging than others, the further along you go, but you can do it," says Olivia.

Although Teresa enjoyed her conversation with Olivia, she still hadn't made up her mind to talk to her father. Teresa told Olivia that she would speak to her brother Nate about going to see him maybe during the Christmas vacation.

"I'm not making any promises, so don't hold me to it."

"I understand, I won't," says Olivia. "I have to run now."

"Okay, I will let you know what I decide," says Teresa.

Teresa felt good about talking to her sister. She seemed sincere to her. The remainder of the day she spent reading all the while still dismissing the calls and texts from Larry.

24

MARKÉTA, NICOLE AND the rest of the Homecoming participants were on the football field preparing for the Homecoming parade and Homecoming night.

"What type of dress are you wearing?" Markéta asked Nicole.

"A strapless satin bubble red dress."

"Mine is a two-tone white top and red bottom since the school colors are red and white, with the shoes to match," says Markéta. "Are you using your car for the parade?"

"No way. I'm using my dad's car. He has a black Corvette. Your brother is going to drive it. He thinks he's driving me in my car, so don't tell him."

"Are you sure about that? Does your dad know?"

"Oh sure."

"I'll be in a drop top Mustang with Isaiah driving. I hope it doesn't rain."

"Hi guys, are we supposed to meet in the gym?" It was Lorraine Dell who had just come around the corner.

"Hello Lorraine," says Markéta. "I think it's out here, everybody seems to be coming this way."

"Nicole, I was for sure that you would win once the freshmen votes were counted," said Lorraine.

"I felt the same way about you," says Nicole to Lorraine.

"Markéta, I see you guys are coming to church again. Do you remember when your grandmother was an usher?

She used to stop us from talking when we were in the little angels' class."

"You remember that?" says Markéta. "I had forgotten all about it. What were we, in the third or fourth grade?"

"I think so. They don't have it anymore."

"Okay everyone, listen up, we only have a few practices to get this done." It was one of the teachers getting everyone together for the homecoming festivities.

While Markéta and the homecoming participants were preparing for practice, DeMario and Big Mike were riding in his car going to check out on some new basketball sneakers at the mall.

"I see you finally added some bump," says Big Mike rocking his head to the beat.

"Yeah man, I added a new amp and some speakers, I wasn't going to do it, but I got a good deal for them online."

"Sweet, now what about some rims?"

"I don't see it happening right now, maybe later. The rims on here are good enough for me, and besides, I don't have to worry about someone stealing them."

"You got that right," says Big Mike with a laugh. "But seriously, they are some cool little rims on it already if you keep them clean."

As they are driving and listening to music they see one of their classmates, Jonathan Payne, better known as Little Hippie, because he was a small guy that dressed like a hippie. He looked as though he had just got in a fight.

"Little Hippie, what's up wit you mane?" asks Big

Mike as they pull up next to him.

"They jumped me and took my money."

"Who jumped you?" he demanded.

"Them dudes over there." He was pointing at some guys standing on the corner of a liquor store. It was Stackman and some of his friends sitting on his car, drinking beers.

"Hey man, why y'all messing with my little cousin?" says Big Mike as he exits the car.

"Fool, that ain't yo cousin," one of the guys says to Big Mike.

"That's my Lil homie," he says to one of the other guys that he knew.

"What's up wit you Big Mike, who dat wit you, that you, D?"

"Yeah man, what's up Aaron?" says DeMario. Aaron was a couple of years older than DeMario and Big Mike. They all used to live in the same neighborhood. All the while they were talking, Stackman just sat on his car as if he were observing the situation. "Alright mane, he can have his stuff back, but only cause we boys," says Aaron. Once Little Hippie gets his stuff back, he gets in the car. "Man, why didn't you ride the bus?" says Big Mike.

"I missed it, I had to go back to my locker and get something."

"You better watch yourself. These dudes out here are crazy," says DeMario. "You see how Stackman was looking at you?"

"You right. Where you guys headed to? Y'all don't live over here."

"We headed to the mall to check out some new gear for Homecoming."

"Word. Let me roll wit y'all, I saw this mind blowing shirt the other day. You have to come back this way anyhow."

"Okay, cool," says DeMario.

"So, who hit you? Was it Aaron or one of those other dudes?" asked Big Mike.

"It was the one on the car."

"Stackman. I figured it was him. I had a few run-ins with him myself," stated Big Mike.

25

ON HER WAY home from work, Teresa stopped and ordered a pizza from the pizza parlor. She had no intention of cooking tonight. After she has made it home from work, she notices the telephone blinking. Someone had left a message. It was the credit card company. They were calling about nonpayment on the card.

Teresa had racked up almost a $22,000 bill on the card over the last few months, from getting her car fixed, a 10-year-old BMW, which both Nate and Marcus told her not to get, groceries, buying one of those timeshare packages, and dental bills for Mercedes braces. Most of this occurred when she was released from her job the previous summer because of disciplinary action. After listening to the message, she gets a call from Nate.

"So, what have you decided?"

"Nate, for a long time I didn't care if I ever saw the man or even cared what happened to him. You know that I hated the thought of him and how he left us, but I want to look into his eyes and let him tell me himself why he left."

"Sis, I hear you. If that's what you want to do, then we can do it."

"How do you feel about it?" she asks.

"I haven't changed much about the way I feel about the man. When are you talking about seeing him?"

"I'm taking off during the Christmas holiday. How

about then?

"You know I was coming to visit you guys. Let's do it this way, we can fly to Texas that Monday. Then leave out and travel back to your place for Christmas, I wanted to drive my Trans Am down, but that's okay, and don't worry about the plane ticket or hotel."

"Are you sure Nate? That's a great deal of money."

"I got a lot of money," says Nate then he started to laugh. " And besides that, you've never been out west."

That was true. She had never been out of the south. "Guess I can't say you're my only sister anymore," says Nate.

"She seems to be down to earth, at least that's how she comes across on the phone and she's going to school to be a doctor."

"That's another reason I could hate that joker. That could have been you or me."

"I was thinking the same thing when she was telling me that."

"Are you going to speak to him before then?"

"No, I told her when I speak to him it has to be in person."

"Same here," says Nate.

"She has a profile on the internet."

"I'll check it out later. I got to go, Sis."

"What, one of your knuckleheads coming over?"

"You know you need to stop that," says Nate. "Don't clown me."

By the time Teresa got off the phone with Nate, all

the children had made it home and were eating pizza. Her mind went back to the telephone message about the credit card. She remembered listening to the woman on the phone about the timeshare in Florida. She had made it sound so great, so she bought it. She only used it one other time to go to Myrtle Beach. At least all this was on one credit card which was a little better than having all those credit cards with outstanding balances.

"So Markéta, do you have all the stuff you need for the Homecoming?"

"Yep, I think I have everything. They gave us a list and a schedule, so I should be good to go," says Markéta. "Are you going to make it to the parade?"

"Yes, I took Friday off. I don't want to miss anything."

"Can we come too?" begged Mercedes.

"I'll check you guys out of school early."

"We are going to a parade?" asks Carlos. "It isn't Christmas yet."

"It's a homecoming parade for the school and I'm in it," says Markéta. "It's two days away."

"So, Mom, have you talked to your dad?" asked DeMario as he is eating.

"No, as a matter of fact, the week of Christmas, me and Nate will be flying to Texas to see him and our half-sister, so you guys will be in charge," says Teresa pointing at DeMario and Markéta.

"You won't be here for Christmas?" inquired

Mercedes.

"I'll be back that Wednesday evening."

"When will you fly out?" replied DeMario.

"That Monday before Christmas," answered Teresa. "You guys can find Olivia's information online." She gives them the internet information about her sister.

After dinner, Teresa goes to her room to take a shower. Afterward, she gets dressed and comes out of her room with a Bible in her hand preparing to go to Church.

"Mom, where are you going to?" asked Mercedes.

"I'm going to Bible study tonight," remarked Teresa.

"I want to come too," insisted Mercedes.

"I want to go to church too!" hollered Carlos. After hearing all the commotion, DeMario comes into the hallway.

"Mama, did you say you were going to church tonight?" he asked.

"No, it was a last-minute thing. I think I need to go to church more than just on Sundays."

"Mom trying to get her church on," teased Markéta as she came out of her room snapping her fingers and dancing.

"See Markéta, you know you wrong for dancing like that. Carlos, have you taken a shower yet? If not, you better hurry if you want to come with me. Fifteen minutes and I'm leaving."

"I would go with you, but I have to finish up with my homework," explained Markéta.

"Yeah, right," says DeMario.

"What's your excuse?" snapped Marketa.

"Look, you guys are worse than the little ones." After Carlos has taken his shower, the three of them go off to church. Riding in the car, they are listening to, "If it had not been for the Lord on my side," on the radio. They each go to their respective classroom once they arrive at church. Tonight's subject was about letting go of the past and not letting it dictate your future. The speaker explained how we sometimes allow ourselves to have a victim mentality. In turn, that gives us an excuse not to achieve.

The speaker moves on to say, with God, we all get a clean slate each day He gives us life, so stop being a victim of circumstance and take control of your life. Quit feeling bad for yourself. If you don't like what's going on in your life, then make modifications. You and only you can decide how to live your life best.

As the speaker was talking Teresa was analyzing her life. How sometimes even she would require some aid from others, even though she never let it show. Heeding to the speaker, she realizes that God put us all where He wanted us to be at the time He wanted us there. The suffering of some of the people in the Bible was far greater than what she was going through. At least she had a roof over her head, and although not the best occupation, at least she had a job. Some of her friends didn't have one and all of her children were in good health.

26

HOMECOMING DAY HAS finally arrived. The students are in the gymnasium enjoying the festivities. Today is just a half day of school. Afterward, the students are let go and the participants are lined up at the school house for the parade that will start at 2 pm. Markéta is in her Mustang with Isaiah. Nicole is in her father's Corvette with DeMario, waiting for the parade to start.

"If it gets any hotter out here we'll close the top," says Nicole fanning herself.

Teresa, her children, Aunt Janice, and Ms. Lillie have all found a spot under a shade tree. "This is why I wanted to come early," she tells them.

"I hope they start on time," says Aunt Janice.

"Me too," echoed Ms. Lillie.

"We still have to wait a spell," says Teresa. "That's why I brought some water."

After a short spell they could hear the band coming up the road.

"I can hear it!" shouts Mercedes.

"Me too!" yelled Carlos. They see the band and the cars lined up behind them. The participants are waving as they pass by.

"I see Markéta! I see Markéta!" screams Mercedes. They can see Markéta with her name draped along the car as they pass by. Markéta waves at them. A couple of cars later,

Nicole and DeMario wave at them.

The last vehicle to pass by is Lorraine, the queen, with her escort, waving at all the people. After the parade was over Ms. Lillie treated everyone in the car to some ice cream. After that, Teresa drops off Ms. Lillie so that she and the two youngest kids can spend some time with Aunt Janice at her house. Later that evening, everyone is back home and preparing for tonight's game and the halftime ceremonies. Teresa is doing Markéta hair.

"Aunt Janice isn't coming out tonight?" she asks her mother.

"No, she says she saw enough today. Am I taking you to the game?" says Teresa.

"I'm going with Vanessa. She'll be here in a few minutes."

"Don't you want me to take you in that dress?"

"Mom, I'll be okay."

"Okay, be careful out there, a lot of traffic tonight. There may be some drinking and driving involved. I'll see you when we get there." DeMario comes out of his room.

"Boy, what is that you got on, cologne?" laughs Markéta.

"It smells good, doesn't it?"

"Oh, it smells," says Markéta. She and Teresa both laugh.

Everyone eventually made it to the game. The stadium was filling up. Teresa and the kids find a place next to Marcus. He had promised Markéta that he would be there tonight.

"I guess you kept your promise."

"I always do," says Marcus. Teresa sees Chantel and waves her and her son over. "This has been a busy day, to say the least."

"I bet it has," says Chantel. "They tried to work us like a dog today with all those people checking out."

"What's new?" mumbled Teresa.

At halftime a portion of the field was lined off with a red carpet as they called out the different names from the different classes. Cheers rang out from their family and friends. Mercedes yelled as loud as she could once Markéta's name was called. Teresa was taking pictures and recording the activities on her phone.

After the ceremony and the game was over, Teresa spoke with Markéta and DeMario for a few minutes, telling them how proud she was of them today. She took a few pictures of them with their escorts. Afterward, she took Mercedes and Carlos home.

27

MARKÉTA AND HER friends made it to Graffiti's as well as DeMario and Nicole. They were enjoying themselves along with the other students. While talking to Nicole, DeMario glanced over her shoulder to see Big Mike, the twins Isaiah and Isaac, Little Hippie, and a few others at the far end of the parking lot in some commotion.

"I wonder what's going on over there," stated DeMario.

"Who knows," says Nicole. "I saw Markéta and Vanessa over there a minute ago."

"Come on, let's go see what's going on." As they were making their way toward the crowd, DeMario could see Big Mike pulling someone off Little Hippie. That person reached into his pants and pulled out a gun and started firing toward Big Mike. Everyone started running in all directions. DeMario could now see who the shooter was. It was Stackman. Stackman ran and jumped in his car and sped off.

Someone was lying on the ground. It was Isaiah. That's when the screams elevated. It was his sister Markéta. She got to Isaiah before he did. Markéta was crying uncontrollably, stroking Isaiah's face, telling him to wake up, but he was already dead. His head rested on her lap. Her dress was stained with blood. DeMario tried the best he could to comfort her, to no avail. Big Mike was on the ground too, but he wasn't dead, only shot in the arm.

Police sirens sounded off in the distance. A crowd had gathered around Isaiah's lifeless body and nearly everyone was crying. Isaac was next to Markéta on the ground lying across his brothers' body and crying uncontrollably. Someone told Shirley that she'd better leave here and go home. By the time the police had gotten there to cordon off the scene, someone from inside Graffiti's had brought out a tablecloth to cover up Isaiah. DeMario pulled his sister away from Isaiah. She was still crying as DeMario and Nicole escorted her away. The police were questioning different people who were still crying. Parents began to show up on the scene. It was pure chaos.

DeMario learned that the situation started because Stackman was still upset about the incident with Little Hippie. This situation magnified when he thought Little Hippie was smoking some of his marijuana with his sister Shirley. Finally, everyone is allowed to leave. Nicole told DeMario she would call her father to come and pick her up.

"D, why does this keep happening to us?" asks Markéta on the drive home.

"I don't know," he says, shaking his head.

"Why did he have to kill him?"

"I don't know, Markéta. He won't get away this time."

She hadn't yet mentioned the dress. She must really be hurting, he thought. When they got home, DeMario told Teresa everything that had happened tonight. Teresa could only shake her head. *Here we go once more, another senseless death, this time, it was a kid* . She couldn't imagine what his kin must be experiencing. She gave Marketa a long hug as she cried in her arms with the dress still on. That night as she prayed, she prayed that none of her kids would die before her and that she would always be in her right mind until the end of her days.

A few days later at Isaiah's funeral, there were tons of weeping from both students and parents. A couple of his classmates spoke about him, as did some of his past and present teachers. Marketa could only sit in silence as the service was going on.

Upon returning home from the funeral, she just sat in her room and watched television. It was a few weeks before she could smile and laugh again. Teresa could still tell she was hurt inside. Thanksgiving had come and gone. It was now almost time for Christmas. The kids were excited and so was Teresa. It was finally time for her and Nate to go see their father and sister.

28

THE KIDS DROPPED Teresa off at the airport and said their goodbyes. Teresa checked her bags in at the counter. At the security check they made her throw away her water and her body lotion. That aggravated her somewhat. Had she known that she couldn't take them on the airplane she wouldn't have brought them.

This would be her first time flying in an airplane. She wasn't afraid, but she felt some goosebumps on her arms as she sat and waited to board the plane. Was it the anxiety of leaving her kids behind or the anticipation of meeting her father, whom she hadn't seen or spoken to since she was around four years old? She and Nate was flying into Houston, getting a rental car, then driving to Beaumont. She waited about 45 minutes before her flight was called to board.

She hoped she wasn't sitting next to some whiny kid or someone who would want to do a lot of talking. Her first stop was in Atlanta. It turned out to be relatively uneventful. Her seat was next to the window and the person sitting next to her was an older gentleman who slept most of the flight. She had a layover of an hour, which gave her enough time to figure out how to get around the Atlanta airport.

She got to her terminal in time to catch her next flight to Houston. This time, she was sitting in the middle row in an aisle seat surrounded by a college female basketball team. They all wore their team jerseys. Suddenly, they all started pointing toward the front of the airplane. Teresa looked to see what they were looking at. Low and behold, it was the famous rapper **RAZ N KANE** and his crew getting on the plane heading to first class. That's what the extra delay was all about. He was one of Markéta's favorite rappers.

Nate's flight got in an hour before hers. By the time she got off the plane and got her bags from the baggage terminal, he was already waiting on her.

"Hey sis, so how was your first flight?"

"It was fine, no problems at all. No worries," she stated. "The person sitting next to me slept all the way on the first flight. The second flight was noisier with these college kids on it." She pointed at the basketball team. "And we had this famous rapper on the airplane."

"If he's so famous, why is he riding commercial?" muttered Nate.

"It is his first album," she responded.

"Where is he?"

"Over there." Teresa pointed at the rapper who stood grinning as he signed an autograph.

"This time next year, I bet he won't be signing those autographs. Probably be punching out the paparazzi."

"And I thought I was negative," giggled Teresa. Nate and Teresa get the rental car and proceed on their way to their father's house. She calls and checks on the kids, asking them how everyone is doing, and letting them know that she landed safely and was with their Uncle Nate.

"So, have you figured out what you are going to say to him?" asks Teresa.

"No. I want to hear what he has to say," says Nate.

"In his condition, he may not have much to say," remarked Teresa.

"Teresa, he has a heart condition, not a stroke. He can talk."

"Nate, I'm simply saying ..."

"Sound as if you are getting soft on me," says Nate. "Let's stop and get something to eat. We have almost two hours to go."

"Don't eat too much. I think they will have dinner for us when we get there."

"I don't know those people like that," proclaimed Nate. Nate pulls off the road to stop at a fast food restaurant. He goes through the drive-thru then gets back on the highway.

"So how long do you plan on working as a housekeeper?" Nate asks.

"Hopefully, not much longer." It was then she decided to tell him about her pursuing a degree in health information management.

"Oh yeah? Bet you'll be glad to stop cleaning up behind other people. So, what brought this on?"

"Multiple things. From seeing all those young people on the base, knowing I could do some of the same things they do and here I am cleaning up behind them. I don't want to be an old maid ... literally." They both laugh and then are silent for a few moments.

"I think Olivia decided to be a doctor because of his

condition."

"His condition," says Nate as he was shaking his head.

They followed the GPS to a middle-class neighborhood. Most of the houses were pretty nice. They eventually stop at a nice-looking two-story home with a two-car garage, a swimming pool, and a fishing boat on a trailer parked on the side of the house. Nate pulls into the driveway off the street. Teresa could see that the curtains to the windows were open.

"They must be waiting for us," she says.

By the time they get out of the car, someone opens up the front door.

"Hey, you guys made good time! I know that traffic from Houston sometimes can be terrible." It was Olivia. "We are glad you guys came."

"We are too," expressed Teresa. They hug each other. Nate was getting Teresa's luggage out the car when Olivia offered to help him with his.

"Thanks, but I'll be getting a room in town," stated Nate.

"You don't have to do that. We have enough space," explained Olivia.

"Thanks, but no."

"Okay, I won't pester you then," she replied. Nate and Teresa follow Olivia into the house. When they get inside, Olivia's mother comes into the room.

"Y'all come on in, make yourself at home."

"Thanks," says Teresa.

"My name is Rosette, I don't know if Olivia told you."

"Rose, have they made it here yet?" a voice called from another room.

"Yes, they are here," acknowledged his wife. "He just got out of the shower."

While waiting for their dad to emerge Teresa and Nate could see all the Christmas gifts under an enormous Christmas tree. Happy family pictures on the walls and the coffee table of their dad and his present family.

"Olivia and I will step out for a spell while you guys get reacquainted if you will. I have to run to the store to get some things. Is that okay?" she asks, looking at both of them. Teresa and Nate looked at each other and said they were okay with that. Rosette and Olivia head back out the front door as their father comes into the room. Nate was almost a spitting image of their father.

"Nathaniel and Teresa," he says with his hands raised. He wasted no time diving into his explanation. "I have no excuses to give you guys. What I did to you two, and your mother was wrong on my part. It was selfish. I knew it was wrong. When I left that morning, we had so many bills. We couldn't afford the medical cost and me with a dead-end job. I just couldn't handle it anymore. So, I left, I know there's no way I can ask for forgiveness, so I won't."

Teresa could tell by the look on her brothers' face that he wanted to reach out and punch him or do some other bodily harm to him.

"So, how long have you practiced that speech?" scoffed Nate. "You left a mother and her two kids just because you couldn't handle the situation? The *mother* of your two children! How weak and sad is that, dude? You have no idea what we went through. Did you even bother to find out? You are no different than guys out here on the streets, in my opinion."

"I don't blame you, son, for feeling that way."

"Don't call me son, bruh! You lost that privilege a long time ago," says Nate. Nate is standing up and looking at his father face to face. "But you know what? We made it. Thanks for nothing, *Pop*." Then he walks out the front door. While all this was going on Teresa has said nothing.

"Teresa, do you feel the same way?"

"You know we came here to hear your side of the story, well, I guess we got it."

"Every word out of my mouth is the truth," he stated.

"Did you even attempt to check on us or anything?"

"Teresa, if I said yes, I'd be lying to you."

"So, why did you want to find us now?"

"Honestly, I felt it was the right thing to do. So, I told Rosette and Olivia. With my heart condition, I don't know how much longer I got to live." Teresa was just shaking her head, still looking at all the pictures on the wall of what seemed to be a happy home.

"You know, Mom talked about you for a while, then she stopped talking about you altogether. You broke her heart, you really did," disclosed Teresa. "Nate remembers a

121

lot more than I do. That's why he is so angry with you. Can you blame him for that? He even remembers going fishing, going to football games, and baseball games with you. I don't remember any of that."

"He remembers that? Wow, we went to about seven games a year."

Her father was almost to the point of tears. He was sitting now. Teresa didn't know what to think. It was at that moment the irony of all irony, at least in her mind, the theme for the TV show *"Good Times"* could be heard in the background. She always hated that show because she never remembered seeing any good times on it.

"Teresa, I'm still glad you guys came even if y'all hate me," he murmured.

"Hey, listen, I didn't know what I was going to think once I got here, or what I was going to say. I just wanted to hear what you had to say. We can't change the past. It is what it is." After a pause, she added, "Answer me this; the woman you're married to now, did you know her before you were with my mom?"

"No, no, no. I only met Rosette after I return here," he announced. "I met Rose at the post office. She worked there. Back then, I used a post office box. I became a train conductor and I was always gone on the train, so I picked up my mail there." Teresa stood up to look out the window to see what Nate was doing. She didn't see him, so she opened the door. When she sees him over at the boat, she heads out the door with her dad following behind her.

122

"That's one of the top of the line fishing boats right there," says their father. "The outboard on it needs a little work. I just need to change the shaft on the prop. I hit a rock or something. Rose won't let me take it out anymore with my condition and all. She thinks I may die out there and nobody would know it. I usually go by myself. I like the peace and quiet."

"So, what are your plans for it?" asked Nate. "Just going to let it set-up?"

"I don't rightly know yet. My brother wants to buy it. Don't know if y'all remember my brother Paul, he came up a couple of times to see me. Nathaniel, you may remember him." Before Nate could respond, Olivia and Rosette were pulling into the driveway.

"Well, how's it's going?" says Rosette. "That boat, please take it away. You guys can have it, he is not going out in it no more."

"See, I told you," murmured their father.

"We purchased some fresh fish from the fish market," says Olivia.

The three women make their way into the house with Nate and his father still outside with the boat. "Do we need to get a referee for them?" asks Olivia.

"My brother is a hard sell," Teresa chimed in, looking out the window at the two of them. "I can understand if you guys have hard felt feelings against your old man, but he is glad you came. He couldn't sleep all week once he knew you guys were coming for sure," says Rosette. Teresa offered to assist them with the food.

"No, you sit down, we got it. You had a long day," says Rosette as she was preparing to make a sweet potato pie. Teresa watched them prepare the meal and thought back to when she used to help her mother in the kitchen.

"So, Teresa, Olivia tells me you have two kids in high school. You don't look old enough to have two kids in high school."

"Yes, a senior and a junior. The other two are in grade school."

"They grow up so fast, don't they?"

"Yes, they do." As they are getting the food ready, Rosette commented. "Olivia tells me you're getting a degree in health information management."

"I'm working on it. I still have a while to go."

"Continue on. You'll get there."

While watching them prepare the meal, Teresa insisted on making the salad to which they finally obliged. The phone rings and Olivia answers it. During the conversation, Teresa can see the concerned expression on her face. Olivia retreats to another room to finish the conversation. "That was Uncle Paul. He says Grandma wants to come over to see you guys."

Grandma, as it turns out, was their father's mother. Teresa had gone from not knowing if her father was dead or alive to now knowing she had a Grandmother. She gave an upbeat response, "Sure, why not?" What else was she going to say? The dinner was complete when Nate and her father came in.

"Grandmother and Uncle P are coming over," says Olivia.

While they were eating their grandmother and uncle came over. Their grandmother was a small woman in her eighties. She gave them both a hug and said she was so glad to see them. After seeing the uncle, Nate says he remembered seeing him as a child. With all the commotion going on when offered a glass of wine from Uncle Paul, Teresa took it. She hadn't had a swallow of alcohol since the violent end of Jessie on her back porch. She could use one of those right now.

After many conversations about family and the lost time between them, they learned from their Grandmother that their father's side of the family was originally from New Orleans, and she moved away from there after she got married. Their father sat there intensively engaging their reaction to what his mother was saying. Afterward, Nate decided it was time for him to check into the hotel. They couldn't convince him to stay the night.

"I'm so glad to see you, baby. God is good. I'm happy to have seen all my grandbabies before I left this earth," stated their grandmother.

"Yes, ma'am," responded Nate as he made his way toward the door.

"Hey, man, you be cool," Uncle Paul bellowed. He gave Nate a big bear hug and a pat on the back.

Their grandmother and Uncle Paul stayed a little

longer until they determined it was finally time to leave. Teresa's Father and Rosette asked her if she needed anything. She says no.

"Good night, see you in the morning," says Rosette as they retreated to their bedroom. Olivia and Teresa were the only two left talking at the kitchen table.

"I know you weren't expecting all this."

"It's okay, it wasn't your fault," insisted Teresa. The two talked for a while longer about family and school until they decided it was time for bed. Teresa's room was downstairs in the guest room. After showering and preparing for bed, she sends a text first to Nate to gauge his thoughts on today's events. Then she sent a text to DeMario to see how they were making out. He responded they were fine. The children were in bed asleep, except himself.

Teresa lies in bed and reflected back on the events of the day. Nate eventually responded with a lengthy text. He explained that the people they met seemed to be straightforward, but he still had reservations about opening up to their father. He couldn't get over the abandonment or the way their mother was treated.

29

THE FOLLOWING MORNING, Teresa could smell breakfast cooking. She lay there for a second until she recognized where she was. She sat up in bed and checked her phone for messages. There were none. She then freshens up and makes her way to the kitchen. Rosette was making homemade biscuits. She also had grits, eggs, cut up melons, and both bacon and sausage.

"Good morning. I wasn't sure how you liked your breakfast," says Rosette.

"It all smells good," commented Teresa, sitting at the kitchen counter. "The biscuits will be done in a few minutes."

Her Father could be heard in the front room moving around. "I want some real food this morning, Rose."

"Do you know if your brother is coming over for breakfast?"

"I will call him and see. He'll probably eat at the hotel."

Teresa gets her cell phone and calls her brother and asks him if he's coming over for breakfast. He tells her he's already eaten and will be stopping by later. He's going to visit one of his old army buddies that live a few miles away. After talking to Nate, she calls home. Carlos answers the telephone.

"Hey, Momma, when are you coming back?"

"I'll be back Wednesday m. What are you and the

others doing?"

"I'm playing, Mercedes is watching TV, Markéta is still in the bed, and D is gone to work."

"Are you behaving?"

"Yes ma'am. Mercedes keeps trying to tell me what to do and I don't like it."

"Okay, behave now. Love you. I'll see you soon."

"Okay, bye Mama," says Carlos as he hung up the phone.

"So, what are we doing today?" says Olivia as she makes her way downstairs. "Is the food ready? Hey, good morning, did you sleep okay?" she asks Teresa as she grabs a piece of bacon.

"I slept longer than usual, so I had to be tired."

"The biscuits are done," replied Rosette as she took them out of the oven. They all sat around the table except their father, who ate in the front room. While they were eating Rosette explains, "I do volunteer work at the nursing home with another member of my church," she told Teresa. She talked about how they share the word of God with the elderly people they meet, how they are receptive to them, but most of them are just glad someone is there to talk with them. "Some of them have no one to talk to but each other. Their families in some cases, just put them away." She shakes her head sadly. "So, we go over, pray, and spend some time with them."

"Olivia, bring me another plate in here, would you?"

"Okay, bacon or sausage?"

"He gets neither," warned her Mother. "He only gets turkey bacon," she pointed to the dish that had the turkey bacon in it.

"Come Christmas, I'm eating some real food," called her father from the living room.

"I'm going to the grocery store for the Christmas dinner after I leave the nursing home."

"Mom, I can do that for you if you want me to. That way you won't have to," says Olivia when she returns to the kitchen.

"Do you know the difference between a turkey and ham?"

"See, now you got jokes," replied Olivia to her mother. "Teresa, you want to come? Or you can stay here if you like."

"Sure, I'll go with you, just in case you can't tell the difference between a ham and a turkey," says Teresa. They all laughed.

After both of them got dressed and cleaned up to go, Teresa texted her brother to tell him that she and Olivia would be out shopping. He texted her back and said he probably wouldn't be back until that evening.

Teresa and Olivia spent the following few hours shopping for Christmas. At one of the grocery stores, Teresa noticed Olivia carrying some bags. "Why are you carrying those bags?"

"It's because some cashiers have a tendency to lick their fingers to open the bags and that's just plain disgusting to me. Putting their dirty hands on my food. I don't know where their hands or mouth has been!"

"You know, that's a good point," says Teresa nodding her head in agreement. They put the groceries in the car and decided to take a bit of a break.

"I know I've said it already, but I'm glad you came," says Olivia. They sit down to take in a coffee shop. "Honestly, I didn't know how I would feel coming here. My emotions are all over the place, I didn't know what to expect, good or bad, but I felt deep down inside I had to come."

"Once I found out I had a sister and brother, I had to find you guys."

"So, how did your Mom feel once she found out about us?"

"You know, my Mom always felt like there were something more to Dad. At times, certain things about his past would come out. My Grandmother and Uncle Paul knew about you guys."

"So, what made him decide to tell you all?"

"Well, we were watching this show one night about a set of twins that didn't know the other one existed, and it just progressed from there. I stated it would be amazing to have a twin and Dad just blurted out that I have a sister and brother," says Olivia. "Both my Mama and I were surprised. He went on and told us everything. He says he left because your mother had begun to be sick a lot. He didn't know what to do, and she didn't want to move to Texas. He says he didn't tell us, especially my Mom, because he was afraid of

130

what would happen."

"Did your mom feel betrayed?"

"I'm not sure, my Mom is funny that way. Some things from his past, he just never revealed."

"And you?"

"I was shocked. I think I was more concerned about my Mom than me." As she was listening to her sister talk, Teresa recalled the days when her mom was in and out of the hospital when she was a little girl.

"Can I ask you a question?" asks Olivia.

"Sure."

"Do you hate him?"

"The more I think about it. I can't hate a person I've never actually known. I only remember so much and that is bits and pieces. Yes, what he did was wrong; there's no doubt about it." There was silence between the two for a few moments until finally, Teresa spoke. "I'm glad to have you as a sister."

"Aww, that is so sweet of you. I feel the same way too," proclaimed Olivia. "Well, we better go back home. Mom should be back by now."

"Sounds good to me." While riding back to the house, Teresa gets a call from Nate.

"What's up, sis?"

"We are on our way back to the house now. Where are you?"

"On my way there too. See you in a few."

"Okay, bye."

By the time they arrived at the house, Rosette was already there. After putting up the groceries, Olivia and Rosette go upstairs to see the clothes that Olivia has bought. Teresa stayed downstairs in the front room with her father watching television. Teresa realized she hadn't spent much time with her dad.

"Tell me, how are your kids? You have four, right?" Her father broke the ice.

"Yes, I have four children. Two boys and two girls. The oldest is a senior and the youngest is in the third grade."

"Teresa, what is your honest opinion of me?" Teresa thought about it for a second.

"Why do you want my opinion? It won't change anything. You have to live with what you did." At this point, Nate could be seen pulling into the driveway.

"Nathaniel have any kids?"

"No."

"How's your Aunt Janice doing?"

"She says we shouldn't come to see you."

"You know, we never got along." By now Nate is coming into the house.

"Hey."

"Hey, young man. You don't mind me calling you young man, do you?"

"You can call me whatever you want," says Nate while shrugging his shoulders. "Just don't expect me to call you Dad, Papa, Father, none of that."

"I can understand that."

"No, you can't understand that," declared Nate.

"My dad passed away when I was young," says his father.

"And yet you still left us. Get off it, man," proclaimed Nate, shaking his head.

"Okay, we aren't getting anywhere with this back and forth," says Teresa.

"Let him get it off his chest. I need to hear this." Rosette and Olivia could be heard coming down the stairs.

"Nathaniel, can I get you anything?" asked Rosette.

"No ma'am," insisted Nate. "I'm good, thanks."

"Well, I'm going to get busy baking these cakes, so we can all sit down and enjoy one another."

"Mom, you need some help?"

"No, I got it, thanks."

While Rosette was in the kitchen, the rest of them was in the front room watching a Christmas movie. Teresa and Olivia began talking about things related to the medical field.

"I have some books, CD's, and notes that you can have."

"Are you sure?" beamed Teresa. "Because I will take it all."

"Sure, I don't need them anymore. Most of it I have on a document file, anyway," Then she turned to Nate. "So, what do you do in the army?"

"I'm in the infantry."

"So, you are a grunt?" says his father.

"You must be gone a lot."

"You get used to it," he nodded sagely. "It's not so great for guys with families sometimes." Olivia began asking Nate more questions about his job.

"What time does your flight leave tomorrow?" asks Rosette as she comes into the front room.

"We have an 11 o'clock flight," says Teresa.

"If you guys don't mind, can we pray this evening before you leave?" They all looked at one another.

"It's fine with me," says Teresa. After finishing up in the kitchen, Rosette had them all stand up as she says a prayer about love and forgiveness. After the prayer, Rosette read some scriptures from the Bible. Then she asked each one of them did they have any words or thoughts. "This is not easy for me to say. I can't speak for my brother, but I'm glad I came."

"We are happy you came too," says Rosette. "And I'm sure my husband is too."

"I'm glad y'all came," says their father.

"Well, it's getting late, and y'all got a busy day tomorrow." Nate stood up.

"I enjoyed your company," he says to Rosette and Olivia. Then he turned to Teresa. "I'll be here early in the morning."

After Nate had left, they all went to their respective rooms. Teresa packed up her things, so all she had to do the next morning was get up and go. Before she knew it, her

134

alarm clock was going off — time to get up. Rosette had already prepared breakfast.

"You didn't have to do that."

"I know," says Rosette. "You can't leave here on an empty stomach." While she was eating breakfast, the doorbell rang. It was Nate. Rosette asked him had he eaten yet. He says no. "Come on in and eat young man."

"Okay, thanks," responded Nate.

Their dad and Olivia had made it to the dining room and they all sit and eat breakfast together. After breakfast was over, Olivia grabs her digital camera.

"Let me take some pictures before you guys leave." After taking the pictures, it was time to go. As they made their way out the door, Teresa gave Olivia one last hug. "Call me if you need any help," says Olivia.

"I will. You can phone me anytime too."

Their dad reached out his hand to Nate. "Safe trip back home." Nate reached out his hand.

"Thanks."

Rosette, Olivia, and their dad wave them off as they pull out of the driveway. Teresa smiles at Nate. "I see you shook his hand," she says.

"I wasn't going to be rude. Mom didn't raise me that way."

"Oh, okay," says Teresa with a smile. "I'm ready to go home and leave Texas." The ride to the airport seemed quicker than the ride from the airport.

"So, was it worth the trip?" asked Nate.

"I think it was. What about you?"

"I'll give you an answer later."

"Yeah, I bet you liked that boat."

"I did like that boat."

"I think Rosette would have given it to you."

After returning the car at the airport and checking in, Teresa called home.

"Hey, it's Mama." It was Mercedes on the phone.

"I know, you still in Texas?"

"Right now I am. It won't be long. Before you know it, we'll be back home. Where's everybody?"

"Carlos is out back, Markéta is in our room, and D is at work I think."

"Okay, I'll see you in a few hours."

"Okay, bye Mama." After about 45 minutes the announcer calls for their flight number. It was time to board. Once they board the plane, Teresa sends a text to Olivia thanking her for all the hospitality. The airplane makes its way down the runway and they are headed back home.

30

O N T H E F L I G H T back home Teresa reflects on the past few days as she strolls through the pictures on her phone from meeting her father, her sister Olivia, Rosette, and even her uncle and grandmother. Nate, who was sitting by her, looked over to see the pictures.

"So, what do you think of Rosette?" asked Nate.

"You know, I think she is nice."

"Yeah, you can tell she is very spiritual, bible scriptures all over the place."

"She seems to be real enough to me, I guess," nodded Teresa. "I like Olivia too. She's a trip. She carries her own grocery bags to the store." She explained to him the reason why. "We went to a store that had the price marked wrong, the price should have been marked for a higher price. She tells them it was their fault and got it for the posted price."

"Sounds like somebody I know," he says looking at his sister. "Y'all got something in common."

"Yeah, and you look like your dad."

"Hey, don't be saying that."

Teresa arched her brow and turned away.

DeMario, Carlos, and Mercedes were at the airport waiting for their Mom and Uncle Nate to arrive.

"How much longer?" says Mercedes.

"Look at the board. The plane lands in fifteen

minutes," says DeMario. "We just got here a little earlier."
After about ten minutes, DeMario says, "I think that's it right
there."

"How do you know?" says Carlos, who has been
playing a game with his brother's cell phone. "Because the
board says the airplane has landed."

"Now how long do we have to wait?" complained
Mercedes.

"It shouldn't be long now. They are opening up the
door." After another ten minutes has passed, the people are
coming through the door. Finally, they see them. The two
younger children run over to their mother.

"Mama, you were gone too long," says Mercedes.

"I was only gone a few days. Where's Markéta?" she
says as she gives them a hug.

"At home," says Mercedes.

"Hey, Uncle Nate."

"My man, how you been?"

"I'm good," says DeMario.

"D, you almost taller than I am and you still growing,"
he states as they make their way to baggage claim.

"So, how was it meeting your dad and sister?"

"I enjoyed it for the most part," says Teresa.

"What about you, Uncle Nate?" Nate is silent for a
while before he speaks.

"It was an experience I won't soon forget. They were
happy to see us," he says.

138

31

AFTER THEY HAD made it home, Teresa could see that the kids had added decoration to the Christmas tree and more gifts.

"Where did all those gifts come from?"

"From D, my Dad, Ms. Lillie, and Aunt Janice," says Mercedes.

"That one is from my Daddy," says Carlos, pointing to a gift under the tree.

"Wait! I have a few in my bag too," announced Uncle Nate pulling gifts out of his luggage.

"I have some too. Olivia bought each one of you a gift," says Teresa.

"I can't wait for Christmas!" says Carlos.

Once everyone has calmed down, DeMario tells Uncle Nate that he is sleeping in their room, the way he always has when he visits, and he and Carlos will sleep in the living room on the sofa bed.

The following morning after breakfast is over, Teresa and the girls start cooking the Christmas dinner. DeMario has already gone off to work. He's working the morning shift during the Christmas holiday. Nate has borrowed Teresa's car to check on some old friends and see the old neighborhood.

"Mama, is Aunt Janice coming over for Christmas?" asks Mercedes as she is licking the icing bowl.

"She's supposed to— someone we'll have to pick her up tomorrow morning. I'll probably get D or Nate to get her."

Later that day, after all the food was prepared, and DeMario and Uncle Nate had returned home, they sat about watching Christmas movies and listening to Christmas music, singing along to the melodies.

"Mercedes, play jingle bells on the keyboard," asked Marketa.

"Yeah, Mercedes, let me hear you," says Uncle Nate nodding his head. "Wit yo bad self."

"All right, okay," says a smiling Mercedes as she heads toward the keyboard. Mercedes pretends she is playing.

"Girl, stop playing," says Marketa. Mercedes laughs, but then plays the tune as they are singing along. She missed a note.

"Wait! Wait! I got to start over," says Mercedes, throwing her hands up.

"No, you're doing good," hailed Uncle Nate. After Mercedes was done, Teresa asks them, "Can anyone tell me why we celebrate Christmas?"

"The birth of baby Jesus," says Mercedes.

"That's right! And we give gifts because the wise men brought him gifts, so let's not forget tomorrow why we celebrate." They all nod their heads in agreement. "Okay, little ones, it's bedtime."

"But I want to stay up all night," expressed Carlos.

"Maybe tomorrow night," surmised Teresa.

"It's time for everyone to go to bed, so D and Carlos can let out the bed," yawned Teresa.

"I'm worn out myself," says Nate. "Goodnight." Everyone says their goodnights and depart to their respective rooms.

Finally, it's Christmas morning. The kids are up and ready to open up their presents. When they come into the front room, they notice a desktop computer. True to his word Uncle Nate had bought them a brand new, top of the line, desktop computer with a 22-inch screen. He had put it together during the night.

"Ooh wee," says Mercedes as she races over and sits at the desk. "Mama, now can I get an email. You said once we get a computer I could have one."

"Okay, later today someone will get you an email account," stated Teresa. She turns to DeMario. "Can you go get Aunt Janice?"

"Sure, you want me to go and get her now?"

"Yes, I'll call her and tell her you are on your way."

"I'll ride with you, D," says Uncle Nate.

"Let's finish opening the presents first," says Markéta.

"Okay, you're right," reckoned uncle Nate. After all, the presents were open DeMario and Uncle Nate headed out the door. DeMario notices some rims lined up on the driveway.

"What! Uncle Nate, you got me those rims I told you

141

about on the phone," says DeMario dancing in the front yard.

"Man, I'm going to have them bad boys put on tomorrow," vowed DeMario. In addition to having Aunt Janice over, Marcus was invited by Mercedes to spend the day with them. The guys were outside on the back porch playing dominoes, and watching the football games, while the women were inside. Everyone was enjoying themselves. Markéta was on the new computer with Mercedes. Carlos was playing with his new games.

"It's good to have everyone over on a good occasion," says Teresa.

"I know, right," concurred Markéta.

Everyone stayed up late that night, Carlos and Mercedes were allowed to stay up late during the remainder of the vacation season. Uncle Nate stayed through the New Year's holidays and then he had to return to work.

32

SUBSEQUENTLY, THE HOLIDAYS were over. Teresa is now back at work. The children are all back in school.

Her kids could gauge some changes in her. She no longer bought any alcohol or smoked. One day Markéta asked her. "Mom, you don't drink anymore?"

"I am trying to quit, I don't have a taste for alcohol. I think the last drink I had was in Texas, and besides, I want to be around for you guys a long time."

Teresa had told them over the Thanksgiving holidays that she was going to school to get a degree in the medical profession. At work, she only told Chantel who says to her, "You need to leave here. Teresa, you're smart."

"I should have done this a long time ago," replied Teresa.

"I can't go to college. I have to get a GED first," says Chantel.

"You can do it," says Teresa.

But deep down inside she knew that would be a challenge for Chantel. Her son Tyson was diagnosed with ADHD. He would often go on a tantrum at school and home. Some of the younger teachers couldn't control him and often she would get a call from the school. When Chantel would come over and get her hair done, he would sometimes blow up, until he sees Teresa, then he would calm down and behave. For some reason he was afraid of her. *Chantel is a good person. Sometimes life just gets in the way.*

Today there was an inspection going on, so the past week leading up to the inspection, management was overseeing the housekeepers and maintenance more carefully than usual. Teresa along with the rest of the housekeepers was told to make sure all aspects of their job were done properly and to use their checklist.

"They want us to do all this stuff, but half the time we don't even have enough people," says Chantel as they head toward their assigned building. "I'm thinking about getting me a job at the Mega-Mart or a casino. I'm sick and tired of this. These guests complain all the time about something. Then when something comes up missing, they think we did it."

"Well ..." commented Teresa.

"You know what I mean," laughed Chantel.

Teresa went to work cleaning up her assigned rooms and watching the guests come and go. Some acknowledged her presence and some didn't. One of them told her the maid that cleaned his room didn't leave him any toilet paper. She reached into her cart and gave him the roll, then she says to him in her nicest voice possible, "It's housekeeping, sir."

"Pardon me?" he stated.

"It's called housekeeping. We're not maids."

"I'm sorry, ma'am," he says, somewhat indifferent.

This magnified her desire to get her degree. *There's no stopping me now*, she thought.

She was never embarrassed about her job because

most of the people she hung with had the same types of jobs. Often, she would look in the mirror and say to herself you should be doing better, like sitting behind a desk somewhere, giving orders instead of taking them.

She had been on several websites looking for jobs. Most of the good paying jobs required a college degree. Maybe she should just open up a beauty salon, daycare, or become a Realtor and have her own hours, but then she would have to start all over for those.

As she was preparing to clean up her next room, while opening up the door, she could smell what could only be one thing. The previous guest had thrown up in the bathroom. How she hated this part of her job. It was all on the toilet and the floor and some of it was on a bath towel where they had tried to clean it up.

While she was cleaning it up, she observed a note on the desk that says 'I'm sorry' with a twenty-dollar bill attached to it. She didn't even want to touch the money. This wasn't the first time she had to clean up someone's vomit, especially on the weekend. After the room was all cleaned up, she makes her way over to laundry to turn in the dirty laundry for new ones.

As she is waiting, she takes her cell phone out and goes to a Bible quiz app, and realizes she doesn't know almost none of the answers. *Wow*, she thought. Especially from the old testament, outside of Adam and Eve, Abraham, Moses, King David, Daniel in the lion's den, and a little of the Samson story. *How sad,* she thought. But this will all change. She then gets a call from the housekeeping supervisor. What do they want now?

33

DEMARIO AND CARLOS are on their way home from washing his car when he notices Larry's car parked in front of their house. "What is he doing over here? Mama isn't home." He looks inside the car but doesn't see Larry. "Stay out here," he tells Carlos.

Entering the house, he hears voices, coming from one of the bedrooms. As he makes his way through the hallway, the sounds are coming from his sister's room. Once he gets to the room, he can see Markéta was laying across the bed while Larry was sitting on the end of it.

In a loud voice, he says, "Man, what are you doing in my sister's room!"

"Hey man, it ain't what you think it is."

"Dude, my mama ain't even home." Then he stood directly in Larry's face. Larry attempted to force him away. "All right, stay right there," says DeMario, as he heads toward his mother's room. Markéta sees him go into their mothers' room.

"D, he says he was just waiting on Mama." Then she screamed, "D, don't get that gun!" DeMario went to where his mom kept the gun. He pulled out the bottom drawer. The gun wasn't there. *Where is the pistol?* His mind was racing. Now, Larry was in the hallway.

"You going to shoot me?"

"Get out of here, Larry! Get out!" Markéta was

screaming to him. DeMario ran to his bedroom and grabbed his baseball bat. Larry had made his way out the door. Markéta blocked the door just long enough for Larry to get in his car.

"Girl, what is wrong with you?" DeMario snapped. By now Markéta is crying.

"We weren't doing anything."

"That's not the point, are you stuck on stupid?" he says, shaking his head. "That's a grown man! You don't know what he had on his mind, and you home alone!" shouted DeMario.

Teresa could hardly control herself as she rode home. Markéta had called her on the phone to tell her what had just happened. Thank God, she had removed that gun. DeMario's car was in the yard and Markéta was outside sitting on the porch on the phone.

"Are you okay?" she stated. "Where is DeMario?"

"In the house," said Markéta. DeMario was in his room, sitting at his desk with the bat in his hand. He looked up when he heard his mother come into the room. With a sigh, Teresa sat down on the bed.

"D, baby, you could have messed up your life today."

"Mama, I know."

"Let me finish. I know you were only trying to protect your sister, but you could've killed him. Or he could've killed you, or all y'all could've been dead, and Carlos is right outside."

DeMario raised up his head. "Mama, I know, but sometimes Marketa just doesn't seem to get it. Anything could have happened."

"You know I haven't seen Larry in a while, don't you?"

"Then why was he over here?"

"He was coming over to speak to me." Marketa was sticking her head inside the room. "Come on in here," says Teresa. "You guys know I love you, right?" They both nodded their heads. "Have you noticed some things have changed in my life?" she asks. "I'm trying real hard to make a better life for us all, today at work they said I should apply for one of the supervisor jobs. Me of all people."

"Mama, they did?" says Marketa.

"Yep, but they don't know. I'm trying to get out of there. Ever since I've been going to church and praying more, things have begun to happen for me in a positive way."

"Are you going to accept that position?" asks DeMario.

"I don't know. I'm thinking about it. I still have a few semesters to go."

"Mom, are you going to be a nurse?" says Marketa.

"No, mainly getting patient information, coding, consultant. There are other things involved with it. I think I'm going to like it," she says.

"Will you have to wear scrubs?" burst out Marketa.

"Maybe, I'm not sure. Probably depends on where

149

I'm working," responds Teresa as she is standing up. "So, are we all cool in here?" The siblings looked at one another.

"Yes, ma'am. I'm sorry, Markéta, that was stupid what I did," apologized DeMario.

"You were just doing what a big brother is supposed to do," says Markéta.

"Thanks by the grace of God, I moved that gun when I did," says Teresa. "Okay, I have to get dressed."

"Where are you going?" they ask.

"Oh, I didn't tell you?" she teased. "Marcus is taking me to see a gospel play, any objections?" she says with a smile, looking directly at DeMario.

"No ma'am," says DeMario smiling back at her.

Yes, things were going to be better around here she thought. As she is getting dressed, she looked up in her closet and notices that watch. *Well I guess, I'll be turning that in tomorrow.*